A Gradual Backslide

JEFFREY ELLINGER

ISBN: 0692597611
ISBN 13: 9780692597613

1

Photographs show a happy baby with wispy blond curls, always kind of half-grinning. One in particular, taken by his mother, is of Joseph standing but wobbling beside a toy pickup truck big enough for a toddler to ride. He is in the front yard of the Bethel house, on rented land where Robert Bethel, Joseph's father, farmed near a small town in southeastern South Dakota. In the shade, baby Joseph is large, bracing himself against the seat of the truck to keep from tipping over. His head is larger still, and he wears no shirt, unknowingly showing off a pale belly. The elastic edge of his diaper appears above the waist of his blue jeans, fly unzipped. A grin covers his face.

Not so long after that photograph, Joseph formed his first memories. And as soon as he did, he began to see how his life would unfold. This vision at an unusually early age left Joseph Bethel in a solitary place. Naturally enough, of the personality traits he would develop, he developed worrying first. Even

Brady Walter, the best athlete in the Hudder, South Dakota '98 graduating class of twenty-six students, and one of the most harmless, prompted the other boys at recess in elementary school.

"Bethel worries too much if you're out of bounds. He won't let anything go. Don't let him think he's cool."

And in a way Brady was right, Joseph Bethel did worry too much, but in another way Brady could not have been more wrong. Joseph would never get to the point where he thought he was cool, even when he moved to the Pacific Northwest—a place he'd always wanted to live—and for a short time was with a curly-haired environmentalist who looked the way Joseph dreamed his wife would look, and he had a job that paid good money, or at least more than he ever thought he'd make. It seemed Joseph just was not built for it, not from his very first day.

On those years on a farm in South Dakota, and on how he grew up: with a mother's tender doting and a father's strong hand. And on who he later wanted to be, his father's father, Grandpa Bethel, who owned land and sired children and made things with his hands. Dogs accompanied Albert Bethel through life, and those dogs birthed puppies given away to deserving kids who came as hired help to the Bethel farm in the summers, and those kids, who later worked as insurance salesmen or mechanics or feed haulers, would remember those dogs for the rest of their lives. Albert Bethel was well known by those boys and girls who lived on nearby farms, because when they mowed Mr. Bethel's lawn, he paid them well, as long as they mowed the right way. And they did, because they did not want to disappoint a man like Albert Bethel. They listened well, and could quote with veracity into adulthood his aphorisms, like "dog tough," "Judas priest," and "play the pieyano." They did not replay these sayings with mimicry but, instead, with reverence.

Unlike Joseph, Albert Bethel worked the land and made it fruitful. He drove horse trailers to move sons and daughters into college, backing into spaces only someone with significant trucking experience backs into, and, along with his wife, Gloria Bethel, held gatherings in his humble yet clean home of fifty years, where the women of the family served turkeys and hams and frosted cookies, fizzy strawberry punches and mashed potatoes with flakes of garlic, cheesy egg cracker dip and caramelized bacon-wrapped mini-wieners and butter-horns—fluffy crescent rolls in the shape of a conch—all those tender meats and hearty breads tumbling and turning onto the sweet corn and smooth gravy.

Albert Bethel shook a man's hand as it should be shook, a salt-of-the-earth kind of handshake, a true handshake, one which Joseph wished as he got older could be his own, without irony or artifice or thoughts of anything else. And Albert had married a beautiful woman at a young age, without ever knowing another. When he laughed, he had no other care in the world: his eyes closed, making two slashes, a great pillow of air entering his bulging chest, his upper body a blissful significant barrel.

He provided enough so there would be birthday money for his children, and his children's children, and Christmas presents, too. But to get to that point Albert Bethel had endured years of scratching at the land. Through harsh weather he perdured, not succumbing, even after a tornado ripped off the roof of his house. With the help of other good men from neighboring farms, he rebuilt it with wood from the lumberyard in town.

Growing up, Joseph can remember how Grandpa Bethel attended recitals and plays and basketball and football games, and from Joseph's place in the choir or on the sidelines it seemed like a reward, not for Joseph, but for his grandpa to do such things.

Albert Bethel knew every man and woman within a thirty-mile radius of home. Listening to gossip was the meanest sin he ever committed, but maybe even that was for good because he always went to visit a neighbor in need, whether the local drunk or a lonely single farmer. He visited with men at the county jail too, handing out copies of Gideon's Bible one weekend a month. Grandpa Bethel loved when it came time for his granddaughters and grandsons to put on their yearly Christmas shows at his home—back when Joseph and his sisters and cousins got done up in dress-up clothes and made a cheering triangle and introduced it with "Welcome. To. Our. Show." Even if Joseph's sisters loathed Joseph's performances—consisting of him putting a teddy bear on his head and telling knock-knock jokes—Albert laughed and did not retreat to the basement with a beer. Albert Bethel never tasted booze his whole life and was well pleased with what he'd given birth to. His offspring spread across the sky like stars.

Joseph's father was similar to Albert. He had been a teacher after college at Hudder Public and a part-time farmer, then a banker, all to support the Bethel family. On those early years and where Joseph grew up: the red tractor and its Byzantine engine exposed like ribs of a skeleton. Joseph would sit on its metal seat and pretend to drive, though Dad did not allow his boy to actually drive. Robert Bethel did not want his son getting hurt or breaking anything. Later, when Joseph revisited pictures of himself on the tractor, he saw a happy boy going nowhere, and felt an emptiness, along with the acute knowledge that his hands knew very little.

Sheep on the farm. Joseph and his sisters fed them clover covering the land like a blanket. So sweet, they could pluck it straight from the ground and eat it for themselves. How the coarse-haired sheep, not white but mother-of-pearl, would poke their black, wet noses through the wooden fences to snack out of the children's hands.

They played in the summer. A black tarp would've been a reliable substitute, and has been for less fortunate farm kids, but the Bethel children were blessed to have a brand-name product to slip and slide on. Children from a nearby Mennonite family would come and play, one of them later playing piano in New York, the other reaching heights as a cellist in a nationally known philharmonic, but back then they didn't mind falling and laughing all over the Bethel front yard as the sunlight dwindled over the shelterbelt. Beyond that, miles of corn and soybeans as the moms stood and admired their progeny.

A strawberry patch sandwiched behind the chicken shed. Its steamy black soil, the berries glistening and plump when the rains came. Joseph never contributed much on the farm, though he did pick the strawberries, carrying with him an empty vanilla ice cream pail, walking alongside his mom in her work jeans and long shirt, tugging if he found a particularly juicy one. She would lean down and kiss her boy's forehead.

From the strawberry patch to the chicken shed and the hundreds of chicks, maybe more. How loud they could be. A yellow sea of fluff, arching their tiny beaks for a morsel of food. A communion of voices bouncing off the humid walls. A sandbox, too, between the chicken coop and the unused garage where Dad kept his blue pickup. A country-sized sand-box, the kind a town kid dreamed of. Joseph had no friends, not for miles, and his sisters were at school, but his imaginary friend named Johnny helped concoct entire worlds.

The pigs, their pink hides, Dad talking to Mom about how hard they were to handle. And horses, Sunrise and Sunset, gone before Joseph was born, though their memory lingered in the barn where a saddle hung over a gate. The cats and the puppies and everything else on a farm. This kind of life lasted until the age of seven, at which point the Bethel family built a house on the outskirts of Hudder, a small farming commu-nity with roots in God, light beer, and football. One day, as a young boy, now a "town kid," Joseph turned on one of the two computers inside a square, red brick building. This was his elementary school.

Waiting, Joseph spun around in a wheeled chair. He wore sweatpants and a purple and yellow Vikings t-shirt. Finished early with the "Gold" in his packet of colored reading work-sheets, as well as his daily cursive practice, Joseph waited. The oddly shaped letters, written up on the blackboard back in the classroom, were still being transposed by a majority of the same kids he would see almost every day for the next ten years of his life. They looked up at the board, then down at their sheets of paper, trying to re-create them. With pencils, no pens, as ink could not be erased, they copied letters like the uppercase Q. Particularly strange, that one, like a number and a letter.

Joseph and a girl named The Boy (she earned this name later, when she never grew breasts) and a boy named The Hurdler (the story was, for as long as anyone could remember, that he'd jumped over a car) had completed their cursive practice and their reading assignment. That day, it dealt with the invasion of killer bees, which, based on the graph in their packet, would be leaving Mexico and going up through the Texas Panhandle, then through the arid flatness of Kansas and Nebraska, hitting Hudder by the year 2000.

That future seemed an eternity away to Joseph, so even if the killer-bee invasion became real, he'd be old enough by then, he probably wouldn't care. More than anything else, Joseph was proud to be in the room with the computer beside the librarian's office, a dusty space with ancient desks stacked on top of each other. The Boy, a white-haired girl, still typed. Joseph just watched, waiting to play a game stored on a floppy disk. Around the corner and down the hall was another classroom, with a partition dividing it into two smaller classrooms. And while Joseph was okay at understanding the reading assignments and pretty good at spelling the answers in cursive, it was multiplying, and especially dividing, that he struggled with. So he did the math flashcards—addition and subtraction, multiplication and the dreaded division—and worksheets and played a variant of Space Invaders in the room with the slower kids. Stigmatizing but livable, to be bad at math. Joseph could get around it. A lisp, though, that he could not so easily navigate.

In between the upstairs and the downstairs of that brick elementary school was an office where Joseph spent more time than any other in his class. The blind on the one window in that room folded up like an accordion when all the schoolchildren went, one by one, once a year, and sat next to a reel-to-reel machine. They put on a pair of plastic headphones and listened for higher- and higher-pitched beeps.

"Raise your arm when you hear it," a proctor would instruct.

Joseph always felt like he did a pretty good job at those tests, but he could have been exceptional at hearing the beeps, or deaf. It was never revealed to the children how well they did, as if it were something the FBI carried out in the '80s to discover those who could one day lead the country into an era of clandestine hearing-based espionage.

Other than the covert tests, it was unknown to most of the other children what happened in that room. But Joseph knew, as did Kim Darling, a classmate who had considerable trouble enunciating her R's. This is where the speech therapist came from Sioux Falls every Thursday to try and temper, if not cure, the afflictions they were born with. It was just that, in the minds of the other children, they didn't talk right.

The exercises with flash cards taxed the limits of what Joseph's mouth could do in congress with his tongue. He wanted badly to not go, and he would have resisted going, if

the choice had been available. Even if it meant being unable to pronounce "statistics" or "thesaurus" for the rest of his life, he would have done it.

But it wasn't up to him; little was, at that age. Until fixed, Joseph would know the range of emotions afforded to a child born with a lisp. Even after curing the impediment, he would.

2

In the years Joseph worked on his speech, he also got used to town life: riding a bike on paved streets, having friends just up the street, hearing the six o'clock dinner horn that everyone in town heard. In this time, Joseph's eighth year, his mom decided to have a party for her son.

"It just doesn't seem like he has many friends," she said, and she had a perm then. It was the style in the late '80s. "We should have a party."

"Yeeeah," Dad said, changed out of the suit he wore for work at the bank and into a pair of stretchy shorts and yellow t-shirt, not as fragile as it would become in later years. Eventually, it became as thin and light as gossamer.

It was a yes, but the party would not be held in the Bethel home. Dad did not want the carpet or the backyard sullied. He grew up on the farm with a mother who dried their clothes on a wire, fastened with clothespins in the clean wind, and who baked fresh bread almost every day. That house, for as long as Dad could remember, was spotless, and he believed his, as a grown man, should be the same.

Joseph's mom grew up along a river but grew up the same, and since she deferred to her husband's decisions, as it was the only way to get anything done, they agreed not to have the party at the Bethel home. They told Joseph to invite all his friends, though Mom preemptively called the other boys' moms, guessing which ones Joseph would invite. The ones with new footballs, shotguns, and Bo Jackson jerseys.

At recess days later, out on the gravely basketball court by the school building, Joseph announced it. The cold muffled his voice as he said, "And my mom's gonna make the biggest cake for when we go to Gigglebees."

"Shit, that's cool," a boy named Austin Hart said. An innocuous thing to say, it seemed, though Austin, the shortest boy in their class, with a shaved head at the age of eight, wanted to prove something. There was always something to prove. Joseph slapped Austin's hand, while Jarvis Reed, another in their class, came over and did the same with his larger, hairier hand. Joseph felt the sting of bones and nerves slapping together.

"Yep," Joseph said. "And we all get five bucks in tokens. My mom said we can order as much pizza as we can eat." Someone passed the ball and Joseph shot, but it rattled in and out. "You guys ever been to Gigglebees?"

"Like once a month," Lance Painter said, taking the rebound. It was hard to tell if Lance—wiry, with a mouth of white teeth—was lying or not, but no one objected.

"That's awesome," Joseph said. "I wish I could go that much."

"It's cool," Lance said. "But it's more fun when a bunch of people go, then we can play laser tag. That shit is fun."

"That's really cool," Joseph said. "My mom should let me for my birthday."

"Your mom?" Austin said. "You don't ask your fucking mom to play laser tag, you just play. Shit." Several of the boys laughed.

"I'm supposed to check first, I think."

"Don't be a girl," Austin said, and passed Joseph the frozen ball.

For as long as he could remember, Austin had never passed him the ball. Standing there with it, Joseph made his first adult decision. "Whatever, I'll tell her I'm playing."

After Joseph shot and missed, another boy picked the ball up and shot. It went through the rim and down through the frayed netting as one of the teachers, dressed in a pressed black coat, strolled out of the three-story school building and rang a bronze bell. The brassy noise came over the playground and the kids, who had been scattered, funneled inside like it was a race.

"It's not real shooting," Joseph was pleading with Mom that night after dinner. She cleaned the kitchen as her son squirmed on the floor, as if he'd been shot in one of his dad's favorite cowboy movies.

Mom did it all: washed the dishes, cleaned the counter, put away all the food in containers. She watched as Joseph flailed on the gray carpet—the one vacuumed on Saturday, bumping up against the linoleum floor—and did not say a word.

She kept wiping down the night's spills with a rag that still had some use in it: a couple strands of beef, a sautéed carrot, crumbs of bread, smears of Heinz 57. Sounds of the local news wafted up from the TV downstairs.

"Every other kid is playing. I'll just be watching. Mom, I promise you."

"Joseph, you won't be the only one."

Joseph stood up. Time to take a stand. "I promise I will be."

Mom kept wiping down the island. "We can give you extra money for the games, Joseph. I just don't know what I think of it. I'll ask your father."

What that meant, they both knew, and so Joseph ran to his room. There, he buried his head in his pillow. None of the boys from school would see this, though Joseph wondered, as his light-blue pillowcase became wet with his tears, if they did the same thing in their bedrooms. He just couldn't imagine it.

A knock came, the door pushing open at the same time. Locking doors inside the house was not allowed, not even for Joseph's older sisters. Mom sat near Joseph on the side of the bed and began to stroke her son's hair, brush her hand on his forehead.

"I'm sorry, honey. We don't feel comfortable with you shooting." And she moved in to hug her only son. Joseph couldn't help himself—he knew how comforting it would be—so he hugged her right back.

That Friday night Joseph and the rest of the boys went to Gigglebees in a rented van. Mom picked everyone up individually in town, then in the country at one stop, and they all drove together to Sioux Falls. There in the arcade-slash-pizza-place everyone sang "Happy Birthday"—Joseph's mom the loudest—though several of the boys implied, through sly glances, that it was gay. But they sang along, if jokingly, since putting on a good face meant getting extra tokens from the host, and as the last candle's flame became a puff of black smoke, they clapped. One of them even patted Joseph on the back. It was Brady, the most magnanimous, so it didn't mean all that much. Still, Joseph couldn't help but blush.

Next, the boys—starting to get antsy—offered their presents, the things their moms had bought. Mom watched with joy as her son opened the gifts. After that, there was pizza and cake. Then, at last, each was given a parcel of tokens, added to their individual stash, and they were released. The ones from families with more money played the games where you could sit down on a "real" motorcycle or in the driver's seat of a "real" car, while the rest played stand-up games with recognizable characters from Saturday morning. Quickly enough, a few of the boys ran out of tokens, especially the poorer ones lured in by the expensive games. It was then up to the boys with an abundance to take requests for "just one more." Joseph loved it all, every once in a while running back to the party room to thank Mom for such a good time. On one of these excursions, he told her it wasn't so bad to not play laser tag.

"Besides," Joseph said, "no one's playing."

"I'm glad, honey." And she kissed her son on the forehead.

"Yep," he said as he wiped it off. "Going back out there."

Waving, Joseph bounced his way to a machine and put in another token without thinking. He played several more games, and at the end of the last one noticed he saw only strangers. So Joseph raced through his final credit, wasting a quarter like the son of a doctor might, and proceeded to zigzag through the arcade flooded with blinking lights and seemingly mocking sounds. He went by a row of shooting games and heard a police officer on the screen say, "Just say no."

"Where the world?" Joseph said out loud, a defensive grin across his face. He went back to the party room, where no one waited to be taken home, token-less. Mom seemed surprised to see her son. She put down her book.

"Back so soon?" she asked.

"Did you see anyone? I think they might have left."

"No one's going anywhere until we leave, my son. I'm sure they're around."

"Okay, but I'm a little worried 'cause I don't see anybody out there."

In an instant, Mom got up, taking Joseph by the hand. They walked by the same places and looked with the same ignorance. They passed by the laser tag room again, and this time Joseph happened to look through the window. He thought he saw Jerry Molder, a boy in his class with the build of a weightlifter, already at their age. Then he was sure of it: there was Austin Hart, with his signature, butt-in-the-air sort of run.

Mom already knew, she had seen, and though she'd told herself before getting there, and had agreed on it with her husband, that Joseph would not be playing laser tag, she took her boy by the hand, deciding in that instant to forgo pacifism. On the short hurried walk to the desk she rummaged in her purse, searching for her checkbook, and at the counter asked,

"How much does the game cost? My son didn't know they were playing."

Joseph stood next to his mom. He liked to ask when he'd be taller. Every Sunday, rising next to each other after the benediction, as the swell of the organ triumphantly played the congregants out, they'd go back-to-back and compare.

"Sorry, ma'am," the pimpled attendant said, "can't let anyone in once the game starts."

"Oh, I'll pay whatever the full price is."

"Sorry." And he pointed to a sign on the counter. "Can't do it."

In the next moment Jarvis opened the door of the laser tag room and the rest of the boys who would always be connected to Joseph, by the biographical fact that they were all born at approximately the same time in history in approximately the same area of the universe, filed out behind: Austin, Brady, Josh (The Hurdler) Cornish, Langley Travis, Lance Painter, Jerry Molder, and the son of a well-known dairy farmer, Cody Fuchs. All of them sweaty and excited.

"Fuck," Lance said. "I shot the shit out of you." Lance did not see Joseph's mom.

"Lance," she said firmly. To be scolded by another parent, how much worse it is than your own. Lance, who never seemed to get embarrassed, turned very red. "Now why did you boys not wait?"

"We thought he wasn't supposed to play laser tag, Mrs. Bethel." It was Brady, not sweating. Surely he had won. He always did. "We would've told him to come if we thought he could play."

Joseph was unable to speak. Around him stood the people who mattered in his life, and would matter for years to come, and now they would always be able to look back and say, "You remember that time Joseph couldn't play laser tag and his mom bitched us out? God, what a queer."

"What time is it, Mrs. Bethel?" Jarvis asked. "My mom told me I was supposed to be home by five."

"Jarvis, we have plenty of time. I didn't mean to scold you boys. This is a fun day. Joseph, you can play laser tag." And for a second, Joseph perked up. Though he tried not to show it.

"I don't have any tokens left," Austin said.

"Yeah, me neither," Lance said, though there were bills, scrunched in his pocket, along with a visible load of tokens in his Hudder Horns coin purse from First Federal Bank, a flexible maroon-and-white one opening in the middle.

"I don't either," Langley Travis said, and he, even at that age, seemed ragged, and smelled as if he'd just gotten done with pig chores. "I wasn't even supposed to spend that much money. Do you think you could take me home, Mrs. Bethel, I'm not feeling good."

Joseph spared himself any more lies. He went and sat in the party room as the rest of the boys cashed in their tickets and got their prizes: cap guns, glowing Frisbees, Nerf footballs, things to be stored away in a closet for years and only taken out in times of nostalgia, while back home over Christmas break or Thanksgiving.

The two in the front seat were quiet on the drive home. The rest seemed happy, noisy at times, while at others a kind of repressed din came over the van as they whispered in the back seats. When the sugar eroded, and the fullness of their stomachs overcame them, they rested their heads on a window, or on each other, though if one of the boys happened to do that, it was something they would never admit. Joseph did not say a word. It broke his mom's heart, he sensed, but he stayed silent. Talking to her would only compound things. Joseph's eighth birthday started as something promising and dissolved into solemn disappointment. It would seem to be an accurate image, a daguerreotype reflecting Joseph Bethel's life. If someone had given him the negative, he might have been able to tear it up and erase it from his memory. But no one changes anything. Time moves forward. So the day lingers, and Joseph lives, whether well or poorly, with its lasting effects.

3

Between his third-grade year and his sixth-grade year, Joseph grew what adults would affectionately and privately call "a little gut." That paunchiness might've been the most recognizable difference in those years, though it was not the most important, as Joseph would soon enough be a solidly built man. His lisp diminished and was hardly noticeable by the time of graduation at Hudder Public.

After high school Joseph went off to a college a few hours north, still in South Dakota, and found God. Or, as it was preached in the groups Joseph ran with at his land-grant public school, God found Joseph. No girlfriends for Joseph, as it was in vogue—after a book on Christian dating became wildly popular—to save yourself for marriage. Purity would be the reason Joseph gave himself, though the real reason? He was deathly afraid of sex. Handsome enough, Joseph grew thick hair then, and was tall, with long arms and legs, strong from playing sports in high school. But any interest from the opposite sex went over his head, and he focused on his schoolwork—not taxing, as he had chosen the ambiguous field of psychology—and his readings of the Bible. When the four years of higher education came to a close, Joseph moved home with his parents to figure out a vocation. The only thing he knew for sure is that he wanted to serve God. More than that, he wanted a wife. A few months went by and he found a job at a group home, and, if all went to plan, the group home would employ a godly female worker who happened to be hotter than anyone Joseph had ever seen.

In that cozy time of hope, right before the evening news in the Bethel home, Joseph had mostly finished packing. A new life waited outside his adolescent bedroom. Youth and its awkward missteps could be left behind. Though as Joseph went through his drawers, making sure he had not forgotten one thing, he couldn't help but sense something taking him by the shoulders and pulling him back. It seemed so real, he even looked. Right then, the music changed over on the portable stereo with the detachable speakers—one used for the last four years of high school and which he would bring along to his new job—to a song Joseph would later remember as the packing-up song. The charging notes gave him momentum and a renewed lightness in his heart. This was, Joseph cautiously felt, the right plan, one preordained before God arranged every star in the universe.

The items being put more jauntily into a green athletic bag—a Christmas present from junior high with a swoosh on the side—didn't add up to much: clothes, books on apologetics and dating, CDs to provide the soundtrack of a new life. A suitcase lay on the floor, and safely in the middle was the most important thing of all, a Bible, with frail pages and real leather covers and his name, Joseph Martin Bethel, etched in all gold caps on the front. All neatly packed, it gave the young man a kind of inerasable pleasure of everything coming together for good. The room looked barren, hardly lived in, ready for whatever storage Mom and Dad wanted to use it for. Only possibilities bore down.

A broad man, shorter than Joseph, wearing no shirt, just a pair of whitey-tighties, had taken up the doorway. His dusky brown hair was speckled with gray, and many of his chest and back hairs were gray too. He dried his hair with a frayed, color-less towel. Joseph took a deep breath and thought of how that towel had been used hundreds of times after hundreds of show-ers in the same house. It was time to move on and buy his own towels.

"You know," Joseph said. "This stuff will fit in my car. You don't have to come along."

"Come on, bud," Dad said, his chest hair fluffier after his nightly hot bath. A distinguished salt-and-pepper mustache on his face. The register of his voice descended lower. "We wouldn't miss seeing your new place out in the wild open."

Joseph's mom would not be coming along, but it was as if she'd be there. As if Mom and Dad had reached joint con-sciousness after thirty-some years of being married. Joseph did not get angry, nor did he put his CDs into the last box any more demonstratively. Instead, he placed them—Goldenwest, Screaming Brittle Siren, MotorCycle—knowing no good would come from getting upset. There was no winning this argument, only prolonging the losing.

Dad wiped away a smear of shaving cream, down where his neck met his upper chest hair. Joseph saw himself in later adulthood with the same hair, and thought, as he had many times already, that Christian girls—the ones who started to marry while still in college—did not want a hairy man. Even if they all said, "It doesn't matter what a guy looks like, it only matters how much he loves Christ," Joseph knew in their heart of hearts they lusted for shorn men with pecs like The Rock and hair like Samson.

"We'll go out and come back," Dad said, ending the silence. "Not a big deal, bud."

"But it doesn't make any sense, Dad, you know that, right?"

At this, a teasing smile from Dad, as if he was curiously bemused by what he'd helped create some 23 years before. "We'll see you in the morning, bud." And he walked out of the doorway and upstairs to bed. With each step, Joseph reversed in age, all the way back to the womb.

A month before, another trip without Dad, one with a destination hundreds of miles in the other direction, to a music festival in Illinois with Marissa Morris. Joseph knew Marissa, since she said so repeatedly on the trip, had a boyfriend. Barely out of nursing school, she was seeing a "really godly guy" from a well-attended nondenominational church in Sioux Falls.

Joseph drove them in his late-model four-door sedan, a reasonable car. A rock band played as he glanced over. The air conditioning sent stray pieces of long blond hair flittering about Marissa's shoulders. She pawed at them, and Joseph thought, once more, what if, what if he had taken her to scripture studies, lingered after praise worship sessions, hung out with her in large groups? Could she have been The One?

"She might have lost the weight," Joseph thought in the car, but immediately prayed to God for forgiveness.

Cruising on the interstate, the sun tanned their extremities. Sounds of the tires on road beneath them, a subtle undertone to the music coming from the stereo, all of it accompanying their discussion on which bands they most looked forward to seeing.

"In order." Joseph unfurled one finger for each group. "Brother Danielson, Five Iron, ZAO. That Ross, or Russ Cogdell guy, or whatever his name is, was all over the place last year. They played that one song that's like a letter to an ex-girlfriend or something?"

Marissa seemed unsure, so Joseph tipped his head down and growled the words, "Dear Tiffany, you've made me, nauseous for the last time."

"Haha, yeah, I know that one."

Joseph was glad—even if they did not belong together—that he could charm an unmarried sister. It gave him the confidence that, when the time came, he'd be ready to guard the heart of the one God called him to love for the rest of their time on earth, and then maybe, in heaven, for eternity, if some theologies were to be believed.

"And Brother Danielson is really, like..." Joseph stopped. The thoughts on Brother Danielson steamrolled his brain: the fruits on Brother Danielson's cardboard tree represented the fruits of the spirit, Daniel Smith's career, exactly how definitive within CCM is it... "I don't know, he's really good. And Five Iron, I wanna hear them play their new stuff. So that's my three. You?"

"Me?" Marissa pointed to her chest, the well-developed one Joseph was doing his best not to notice. "I wanna see Five Iron, too. Stavesacre. And Spoken. There are just so many."

"Stavesacre, yeah yeah, I saw those guys with Project 86 and Living Sacrifice in Minneapolis last year, I don't think you went. But man, Mark Solomon, that guy is possessed. He was staring at everyone. Nuts, Marissa, nuts!"

Marissa giggled and began to play with her hair as it clung like lint to the dress she wore over jeans. "I would've got trampled."

"I don't know," Joseph said, "I've seen you in the pit, I think you would've been fine."

"I like to dance," Marissa said, and, as much as she could in the car, moved her arms as a ballerina might.

"I think what you do in there is more like wrestling."

"It's better than wrestling, Joseph. When I get in there, it's like I'm on a different planet."

"Too many sweaty guys on that planet."

"Aww, it's fun, you should get in the pit more often." And Marissa jabbed Joseph's shoulder, but just as quickly she took her hand back.

The moment came and went and Joseph turned the stereo up. They began to sing along to a Christian band's cover of a Pixies song. Raucously they sang, and both looked and felt assured, as they did, of where they would go when they died. When the song ended, Marissa asked about food.

"Any place in particular?" Joseph asked.

"I don't care. I'm just so hungry." Marissa rubbed her stomach.

"There's an exit coming up." Joseph motioned with his head to a green sign on the side of the road. It offered a smorgasbord of eateries. "We can stop up there."

So they did, and after they got back on the interstate they stopped once more for gas, then once again for supper. On their final stop, in Galesburg, Illinois, they bought a bag of ice to cool their meats, cheeses, and sports drinks. Beer was not allowed in the campgrounds, though that did not matter. Neither Marissa nor Joseph drank.

They arrived on the night before the first official day. Darkness flirted with the acres of crops surrounding them. Going slowly, Joseph drove on a dirt-packed road through a mass of young flesh. Two golf carts appeared, then just as suddenly buzzed by Joseph's sedan. In front of them was a station wagon with a lacquer of stickers on its bumper. To the left, one boy wore a t-shirt that said "Christ is King" instead of Burger King, while the other said "Got Jesus" instead of Got Milk. A pack of youths riding oversized bicycles wore fishnet stockings and long black coats. Many had cut their hair into a mohawk. The week ahead would be for them, and for everyone else—several close enough to tap at Joseph's window—free of parental guidance. The grounds breathed with a palpable excitement. Pockets of college kids could be found, but they were like a single white garment in a washing machine the size of the sea. Teens made up the current and the waves. These youth groups everywhere. Joseph drove around a bend and nearly into a pack of boys following a girl wearing short jean shorts, short enough that if she'd had a woman's body, they could have seen the beginning of her backside. Maneuvering around them, Joseph knew this would be his last year at the festival, unless he found a wife. He was getting too old.

Marissa, quiet, as they looked for a spot to park. Joseph thought, She will never find anything with that gazing far-off stare. Again, he prayed for forgiveness.

"Last year," Marissa said, breaking his petition, "me and some friends camped next to a generator stage. I barely slept."

"I'll have no part of that, Marissa. We're getting too old. Gotta get sleep."

A soft giggle in the sticky car just as a spot opened up near a deserted patch between two tall trees and right near the lake. Joseph drove them down into the depression and parked. Outside, the air hung on them like a wool blanket. Mosquitoes thrumming in their ears, they began to erect the tent. Sans a handy bone in Joseph's body, Marissa engineered the building, though even with one giving the orders and the other doing the heavy lifting, it was so hot that, by the time it was up, they both dripped with sweat. Marissa excused herself to the communal showers, leaving her partner alone.

By himself, Joseph was left to think what would happen when she returned. How would they arrange their bodies? More or less he would be for the first time sleeping in close quarters with a woman. Only once had it happened before, and though he did not like to admit it, he was at an age where it happened for most. Maybe not every night, but on some it really did. Joseph sat down in the driver's seat, leaving the door open and a foot on the grass. The lake was dark. Nature did not seem to care about a virgin who peered out at its waters.

4

To his first dorm room couch, where he is watching TV. Underneath his lofted bed, Joseph glued to a program about people getting real for once in the Pacific Northwest. A commercial was advertising a zit cream when his phone, with the caller ID box separate but attached by wires, rang.

Earlier in the evening, in a dorm room with a large keg in the middle, it had not taken more than a few sips of light beer to find the courage to sidle his way to the upright dresser under the mirror, there, to the ottoman, where she sat. Almost as tall as Joseph, she boasted a full body and a face lightly peppered with acne. Both of them teenagers, she touched his leg. Joseph made a reference to campus living, how the food at the dining hall was "so bad," then, after a passing back-rub suggestion—she was "really sore" from playing softball—they began to kiss, more and more openly in their corner of the room. When they reached a point where they could go no further in front of others, she got up and left, without warning or reason. Joseph did not watch her go, pretending nothing had happened, but he did think of how, when he put his hand between her legs, he felt warmth. Snickering littered the room.

"You like big girls, huh, Bethel?" a freshman asked. Joseph knew the guy in passing. He always slicked back his hair and wore a v-neck shirt and shaved his chest. Two girls in makeup flanked him.

"I dunno about that," Joseph said as he got up, his face turning red. The two girls, who both wore chokers, suppressed their laughter as Joseph headed to the door, which had a poster of a jam band covering it. As it closed behind, he heard laughter. Cruel but beautiful grace notes followed him down the hall.

Later, MTV on, wallowing in the hollow shame, the phone rang, and with it came such a rush Joseph forgot about the guy with the hairless chest and all the hot girls in the world and their black-laced chokers.

"What are you doing?" she asked. It was Sandra. That was her name. Though as Joseph looked out at the lake in Illinois, he was not entirely sure of that. "Are you gonna come down here?"

"What room number?" Joseph asked, quickly aware of what could happen.

"One-oh-five, I mean one-oh-six Y. No, no. One-oh-five Y. I'll be wayyyyy-ting."

Joseph hung up and sped out the door, not bothering to take the time to lock it. The others could play all the tricks they wanted—poop in the bed, take out all the furniture—he didn't care. Once at her doorstep, there in an instant, they kissed. Joseph tasted beer and spearmint gum, and her soft stomach pressed against his flat one. Then, with the door closed behind them, he scratched the nubs of his nails across her back. He was about to say something.

"Don't talk," she said as she bopped his nose with one finger. She sucked on his neck.

It made Joseph want her even more. With the healthiest portion of her ass he could take, he guided Sandra up against the wall. A poster of a young actor as "The King of the World" looked down on them. They moved to her cold floor, and there Joseph pulled down his jeans. Sandra took off her top and black pants herself, then her leopard-print underwear. Joseph went to her, causing Sandra to make such noises he wondered what the next-door neighbor might ask the next day. Something like, "What were you doing last night?" When they got to the point where he thought Sandra was done, Joseph looked up.

"Let me see what you have." Sandra crawled over to it, half-limp. After, nothing completed and her forehead greasy against his chest on the coldness of the floor, Joseph's head filled with thoughts of pregnancy. He couldn't help it. He imagined his parents having to take care of an illegitimate grandchild. Sandra wanted more.

"We should go up," she said, "more comfortable up there."

Rising, naked and dirty, Joseph became hypnotized with the realization. This would be his first sleepover. Since the time other boys started hoping to have sex, Joseph Bethel had dreamed of sleeping, just sleeping, with a woman. He imagined it would be on a wedding bed on their honeymoon, and he would put her down, pure and perfect, holding her after they were done until she fell drowsy, body heat warming them into slumber, his manly frame providing security throughout.

In the dorm room, Joseph gingerly pulled Sandra's bed sheet to their hips, putting his head on the corner of one of her pink pillows. Her breath was fresh on his cheek as she said, "Just relax," and her cold hand gripped his penis. He did not want to start again, so Joseph began to pray, earnestly, for the first time in his life.

"I need You," he silently pleaded. "Lord. I need You. Please, if You can get me out of this, I am Yours. I am Yours until the day I die." And before anything could be made useful, God spoke, giving Joseph wisdom.

"Sandra." Joseph sat up, his head almost touching the ceiling. "I just remembered, I have to wake up early. I'm sorry. I should go."

Sandra did not say a word. She put her head back down on the pillow and rolled her eyes, though Joseph could not see that in the darkness. He gave her a kiss on her forehead, like a consolation prize, and stepped down on her desk and walked out of her room carrying with him his jeans and collared shirt. A dead grunt came as he closed the door, then a louder "Fuck you" as he walked away, but what did that matter? Joseph knew now that he would not be married at eighteen to someone he did not know, possibly with a child he did not want, forcing him into a life he couldn't stand. And as he went up to his room putting his clothes on, Joseph was fully devoted to God's plan, whatever it might be.

In Illinois, Marissa was about to go into their tent, her hair wet from the shower.

"Y'know," Joseph said as he shut the car door, "we've got a good spot here, Marissa. I really think we do."

She nodded. The late-night commotion of the festival rolled down the hill. "Could I use the tent?"

"Sure," Joseph said. "You bet." He turned away and Marissa zipped it open, then shut, checking it twice. And that night they slept snugly in their sleeping bags. No matter how much they sweated, they stayed enclosed, like in separate cocoons.

Back in South Dakota months later, packing done, Joseph ready to make the move. His CDs, DVDs without any sexual content, books and clothes, collared shirts and jean shorts and sweaters, all in their places. Two cars waited in anticipation in the driveway of the Bethel home.

"Last chance," Joseph said, rolling down his window. "You really don't have to come along." But this was vanity, some symbolical last stand.

"Your mother wants me to see what kind of place you're going to have out there," Dad said. "Couldn't miss it."

So without any more objections, the two men embarked, one in one clean sedan, and the other in the same but a year newer. Joseph reversed first out of the driveway, then his father. Into the early-morning amber darkness, out of the silent small town, a loving yet tenuous pair.

5

The O.C. Supertones played as Joseph drove west. Billboards sprung out of pastures, luring travelers to places like the Corn Palace, Reptile Gardens, Mount Rushmore, Wall Drug. But Wall Drug, Joseph knew, was just a gas station. The Corn Palace, a gym. As for the Reptile Gardens, that was for boys in elementary school, not for men forging new lives. At the Missouri River the state divided from the agrarian eastern half to the pastoral western. The interstate cut through the middle and Joseph drove behind his dad, both going a sensible seventy-one miles per hour. It was the right speed for daydreaming.

A month before, days after the festival in Illinois with Marissa, the headmaster of Salvation's Home for Displaced Teens in Sunrise Center, Wyoming, had given Joseph the tour given to all prospective houseparents. Breathe in the clean air and recently cut grass. Birds sang as Clem Bellflowers, a tall, angular man with a protruding middle, talked about the use and history of each building they passed. He went into specifics too.

"Homework should be worked on for an hour every night. You'll be responsible for making sure it gets done." They walked at a brisk pace. Trees guarded the property, and often Clem would spit, then look at Joseph paternally, reassuring the fresh-faced graduate with a twinkle and a smile.

"Correcting behavior is important," Clem was saying. "Set boundaries. Let them know you're in charge. But ensuring their spiritual needs are met, that's the most important thing. The goal of Salvation is to intentionally lead the children under our care into a relationship with Christ. You're going to be the parent they never had."

Joseph heard Clem, so he would not be able to play dumb when later someone asked what could have possessed him to take the job. But it was the freedom of being away from home, the challenge itself; Joseph was sure this was where God wanted him. So he said, "Absolutely, Mr. Bellflowers," like he did after everything Clem said.

Clem spit, like an agreement with the earth, and they looked across the open field. In the distance they could see someone pushing a lawnmower toward them. The figure got closer, and Joseph could tell it was someone his age, probably recently emerged from a Christian college. She had red hair.

The past four years could have been summed up as an exhaustive search for her, and Joseph feared, like a private in the army being asked for one more tour of duty, he would not return from the next frontline encounter. The group home in Wyoming, he had hoped, would act as a fortress against that longing. But then she came closer, and Joseph sensed it coming like an unavoidable tragedy. He wanted to rend it out of his body. But she was very near, and what could be done.

"Karen," Clem said in a glad way, "I've got a young man you need to meet."

Her pale green eyes, Joseph thought: he could stare at them for the rest of his life, if God willed it to be so. "Nice to meet you, Young Man." She had the faint smell of sunscreen. "How's your visit so far? Everything you thought it'd be?"

"Good, I'm Joseph, where are you headed? Off to mow?" It was as if he suddenly forgot the basics of human conversation.

"How could you tell?" she asked, smiling in a good-natured way. "So you're coming to work with us then? You should. Just look around. We've got a great place here." Joseph did, seeing mountains in the far-off distance.

"Let's just hold on, Karen," Clem said. "We can't get too ahead of ourselves, Joseph just got here."

"All right, but he seems like good stock." Karen put her hands on her hips. "Don't let 'em go too easy." The uneven path God paved so far had been smooth and right. "It's good meeting you, Joseph, I hate to do this, but I have to keep hustling, day's wasting. Maybe I'll see you later?"

"Sure," Joseph said loudly, though Karen was not far away.

"Do come back to our little slice of heaven," she said as she put her weight behind the mower. "We can always use more fellas." She kept pushing, without looking back, going toward a green model home Clem had not yet shown Joseph. The decaying buildings, the beat-up mower, the landscape folded in her wake.

Clem shook his finger once. "Quite the gal, that Karen. You haven't met Darrin. I think he and Karen are getting hitched soon."

Joseph tried to appear unfazed by this, but his expression betrayed him. Always he assumed people saw his face as the kind that wanted to be in love.

"But don't you worry," Clem said, spitting again. "We'll get you a nice girl."

Joseph had been caught once more. "I appreciate that, Clem," he said, mounting his most genuine face. "But I'm concentrating on work these days."

"That's good to hear. Let's keep going, it's getting on." But with each step Joseph's plans to marry and one day have green-eyed babies with Karen began to melt, evaporating as he moved further away from where they first met. Joseph did not know her from more than a handshake, but still he was disappointed beyond measure.

But, as he could only describe it later, a miracle occurred. That seemingly unending disappointment lifted, and in its stead a steely, spiritual maturity blossomed, the kind Joseph knew he would need to develop in order to be given a wife from God. To be given a wife, yes, that would only happen when unfettered from distractions and focusing singularly on Him. So it began to seem to Joseph, as he went to bed that night in a moldy room in the basement of a strange house, that Karen's attachment was a blessing. Though her beauty, her mind-numbing beauty, echoed in his heart.

By the next morning, as Joseph returned to South Dakota, two things were true without question. He would come back to work in Wyoming, and the second, the possibility of some-one else as attractive as Karen working somewhere as remote as Salvation was zero. It had to be. A just God would see to that.

6

To be young and in love is good. To be young and in love for the first time is better. To be young and in love for the first time with someone chosen by the creator of everything that ever was is something only a few have known and what it feels like can only be described ineffably. So Joseph was speechless the first time he met Mary Hutton.

She started two weeks after he did in the small town of Sunrise Center, Wyoming, with its clean air and fresh-cut lawns and mountains in the distance. And the thing Joseph remembers most about the first time he saw her is how lucky he was. All the mishaps as an adolescent, the sheltered loneliness of college, had been a mirage. God was real. Mary Hutton existed. Everything works toward good.

Things started well for them. Mary was tall and muscular after playing volleyball at a Christian college for four years, with long, straight dark hair, and she smelled as Joseph imagined his wife would smell, like clean laundry and fruity shampoo. She laughed at his jokes with a head-tilted-back, eyes-closed laugh, one that captured his heart. They saw each other nearly every day. If Joseph worked, she'd walk over to the boys' cottage in the evening, or, if Mary was working, he would leave the Castle—where the single men lived off-duty—and stroll through the protecting forest of trees over to the girls' cottage, and there they would be together, sometimes into the morning. They discussed the difficulty of being a parent at the age of twenty-three to teenagers. They dug into their personal lives. Joseph never told Mary he believed God caused men—a category in which he included himself—to go bald if they masturbated to pictures of naked women on the internet, though he did tell Mary of his girlfriends in high school and college, the ones who never seemed to be The One. Mary described, in detail, Tony Chester, a man who'd attended the same Christian college in Iowa as she, and who Joseph would see in a photo and would always be pudgy in his mind's eye. Tony had been Mary's boyfriend for the previous three years, all the way up until a month before she left for Wyoming. Tony had even proposed, but she'd said no. He was too pushy, Mary said.

"It wasn't what God wanted," Mary told Joseph. It was a line he would never forget.

Winter came and the two dove even deeper into each other's inner workings—their failures, fears, and doubts—but Mary kept Joseph at arm's length, seemingly waiting for a more godly man with a bigger hammer to break her ice. They browsed personal photo albums and talked about their insecurities: the pimples on Mary's chin, which she said cropped up when she was stressed, and his receding hairline, which he said was worse when it got windy. They reassured one another that these blemishes were invisible.

When alone at night, Joseph prayed for hours for Mary to be his wife. Eventually, he couldn't hold off. He had to tell Mary his feelings, if only to express, in part, their true depth. On the evening he officially gave the news, Joseph walked over to the girls' cottage and stammered his intentions as Mary scrunched more into the couch, hiding her face with a pillow by the end, though he managed to say what he wanted to say, that he liked her quite a bit and also wanted to guard her heart.

Mary walked Joseph to the door in kind appreciation after it was done, and he left without a definitive answer. Even still, as Joseph headed back to the Castle, knowing full well his disjointed outpouring had not been perfect and they had not agreed to be exclusive under God in a courtship, without even a kiss goodbye—as he dreamed Mary might want—the conversation happened all the same. And that made Joseph, a man with no further aspiration in life than to be married and in love, float, full of praises like a modern-day David. Falling asleep, he thought, This is why psalms are written.

But as winter faded, Mary grew more uninterested. No longer did she visit Joseph, either on or off duty. He still went to see her, but somewhere in that season he picked up the childish habit of lying on the floor, even while she was on duty, as a silent protest to her indifference. With spring came two new staff, allaying some melancholy.

Gary Simmons grew up in Idaho and could dunk a basketball, immediately propelling him to status as the most popular houseparent at Salvation. The same age as Joseph, Simmons spoke softly and liked basketball shoes so much they filled an entire large closet in his room. Gary helped Joseph enjoy more hedonistic things, like movies with partial nudity, and music with swearing. And Isaac Shore, who came not as a houseparent but as a maintenance worker. A native of Kansas, Shore strolled around campus with his lanky arms and legs and smoked cigarettes when no was watching. He wore wire-framed glasses and could often be seen with a coffee cup. He enjoyed old 8-bit adventure computer games and the poetry of William Blake and knew how to do manly things, like fix a chair, change the oil in a car, and add large numbers in his head. Isaac hardly ever spoke in the morning meetings with Clem and the rest, certainly not with female houseparents present, and that led to the one time, in their year of working together, Joseph thought Mary was wrong about something. She mistook Isaac's shy silence as rudeness. Joseph never forgot that.

Neither of the two new staff classified themselves as born again, like Joseph, but they fulfilled a need for good male friendship. While living and working in such an isolated town, it was no small miracle. Still, many times that spring and early summer, instead of hanging out with them, Joseph lingered wherever Mary was reported to have been, or was about to possibly be, praying for one of the times in her presence to hold a crucial moment.

After nearly a year of working in Wyoming, Joseph in bed, unable to fall asleep. Not praying, he thought of God, how He must know every desire of every person on the planet, back to the beginning of time. Was it out of love He granted favor to someone like Tony Chester, who surely had touched Mary's perfect breasts? There must be a reason, but as Joseph stayed awake through the night and into morning, beginning to hear birdsong outside his basement window, he could not understand why. The story of Job, people argued about it thousands of years after its writing, and what did it tell us? That God punishes men to win bets against old foes? Meeting Mary had not been happenstance. Every decision and move made in the past year went up a direct ladder, and pails of reward got sent down in return. Near dawn, exhaustion came over Joseph, and as he acquiesced to sleep, he dreamed of those pails suspended above, way up in the clouds.

On the afternoon of her final day at Salvation, Mary was given a party at the downtown office. Joseph, unaware, would have settled for one last roller coaster of a conversation, the very same excruciating, terse back-and-forth on what they were to each other that they'd had multiple times in their last months of working together. He might've even accepted something sinful, like being inside Mary. But he got neither of those things, and the chance to grace her with the elaborate goodbye party Joseph planned in his head the second he heard she was leaving never came. Mary left three days before she said she would. A day later, Joseph put in his two weeks.

Back home in South Dakota, Joseph coordinated a package and sent it to Mary's new workplace, to an address given to him by Clem. It was to show that he knew Mary better than Tony ever could: an expensive floral arrangement, quilting accessories—as Mary was an avid quilter—and a burned mix CD with songs by Lassie Foundation and Joy Electric and others that would, if scarcely, show his feelings. Not quite a month later, Joseph received an email, their first communication since Salvation:

Hello Joseph,

The flowers were beautiful and the quilting gadgets are coming in handy. Working at the library is also going well. But, let me say, I was concerned when I got the flowers and the package. It is thoughtful of you to send me things, but it concerns me because I know that you didn't do this for anyone else at Salvation. We are just friends and I don't want any special treatment from you.

When I was in Sunrise I often felt like you based your happiness on how you and I interacted. But I don't want you to find your happiness in me. You won't find it there. The only thing that is fulfilling in life is a personal relationship with God. Every person will let you down in life. God is the only stable, constant, eternal thing that can bring you lasting joy. We've talked about that before. Listen to your family and forget about me and spend time getting to know God better. I think it is best we don't correspond. Please don't contact me anymore.

Sincerely,
Mary

Over and over Joseph read it, and when he got done reading it for the fifth time, he put his head down on his parents' computer keyboard. After some minutes, he looked up at what the keys had spelled. Of course, it didn't make sense.

7

Be a man. Move to Iowa City. Win her heart. Joseph kicked himself for being and not doing as he played video games in his childhood bedroom, with framed posters of famous golf courses on the wall and a band from Manchester, popular in the late '90s. No man coming of age should live like this in his parents' home. Joseph had such desires to win Mary's affection, but telling his mom and dad? Impossible. What would they say? They never talked about sex or relationships.

So Joseph told no one about his aching, and each night went to bed dreaming of moving to Iowa City, finding a job there and winning Mary's heart. Eating free food, playing Morrowind, his plans drizzled into the background, and the easy life began to erode his dreams. Soon enough, he found a job as a child care counselor in Sioux Falls, priming himself for his real move. Working overnights as a child care counselor at a residential treatment home in South Dakota was not glamorous, but at least Joseph could say that after each shift he went to his own place to live his own life. No more sleeping in the same house as the ones he was charged with watching. As well, and thankfully, there was no one like Mary at the new job, no one distracting him from the Bible study he needed to catch up on, at least not until Charlotte Ester.

Home-schooled until enrolling at the University of Sioux Falls, Charlotte Ester sported dark hair like Mary, though longer and dowdier, like the kind of hair a home-schooled girl would have. Charlotte told Joseph she kept chests' worth of personal diaries, and she could recite Kierkegaard and Buechner, even Chesterton, from memory. She wore makeup, while Mary never did, and was more chatty, often instigating conversations by writing long emails while they worked overnights in different buildings on the same campus. Joseph could not get enough of the adoration. He loved hearing Charlotte say how stupid Mary had been.

Their favorite thing to do was to eat breakfast after their overnight shift. Joseph would go over to Charlotte's apartment, and there they would retire to her small couch in front of the television to watch early-morning talk shows. One morning, while straddling his lap, Charlotte in her usual attire—baggy sweatshirt and jeans—she kissed his left cheek and whispered in his ear, "You're so sweet, so smart." She kissed his left ear. "You call when you say you will call." His right ear. "You can quote Anne Shirley." She rubbed against his cheek. "Not to mention you can sing 'Read Your Bible,' 'Pray Every Day,' and 'All God's Critters.'" She blew on his neck, keeping her hands above his waist, kissing the outer rims of his lips. Joseph did not speak, doing his best to fight against overt arousal, so as not to dissuade Charlotte from continuing.

"You pronounce Yeats the right way." She purred around his mouth. "You come to complete stops at all stop signs and hold the door open for me and you can sing like Stephin Merritt." She kissed his right eye. "You said my cookies were good straight out of the freezer." She kissed his left eye. "You like musicals and foreign films." She moved toward his mouth again. "You work a zillion hours a week and you are already practically my boss." She gave him a kiss straight on the lips. "You let me have the remote without a struggle." She kissed with more intent. "You make great birthday cards." Her words became few, and they kissed without interruption. When they unlocked, the taste of her lip gloss in Joseph's mouth, she let out one last sentence. "I don't understand why Mary didn't want to marry you."

Joseph knew he broke a commandment or two with Charlotte, but the combination of the whispers and her warmth gave him an erection mightier than he'd known he was capable of. He was sure she felt it, though what did that matter? They did nothing more than kiss, that morning, or any other. Things went like that. When not kissing, as if teenagers in their parents' basements, Charlotte encouraged Joseph's idea of moving to Iowa City, imbuing mentions of Mary with great importance. She even went so far as to advise Joseph to write a letter, "to get all your feelings on paper." Joseph never did, though they both knew why Charlotte pushed the idea, because it would surely fail.

The chaste affair stopped before long. Charlotte left for Europe to study religion while Joseph kept working at the children's home. He never moved to Iowa, nor did he try to find where Mary lived, though he can remember a time in his life when he wanted both of those things dearly. He wanted to be with Mary more than anything else he would ever want again.

Charlotte gone, Joseph assessed his life. He was not rich, didn't have a great job, and most of his friends in Sioux Falls had, by then, married. As he worked at the group home overnight, playing computer games and drinking pop, he often thought of the lives others might have, full of weekend trips to Canada for skiing adventures, five-dollar coffees with twenty-dollar lunches followed by even higher-priced dinners, new MacBooks, erections for women in long-term meaningful relationships, big-time decisions, screens of missed phone calls, large donations to nature charities, meaningful offerings to important conversations, flights to London and Tokyo and Moscow, high-powered job offers, copies of the New York Times with breakfast in bed after nightly sex marathons, Volvos off the lot and new bedding daily brought in by maids, a lifestyle peppered with attractive people and far-off settings. Maybe not everyone was living that way, but some were. And for the first time since praying the prayer, in a dorm room years before, Joseph desired to be one of them.

Perhaps the internet would be the way to go. Everyone was saying how great it was. Even Joseph's brother-in-law, who acted as a representative for the rest of the Bethel family when it came to issues with Joseph, relayed a story of an older man from his church who found someone from the internet, a wife, even. So Joseph set up a profile on MySpace and quickly enough secured a date at a coffee shop. The one opposite him that afternoon wore elderly perfume, and their conversation was forgettable—for most of the time she talked about visiting Prague—but to go on a casual date seemed like a big step for the still-young man.

Then Joseph met another, an atheist by the name of Claire Hardy, all thanks to Ulrich Bornhoft. Bornhoft worked for the Argus Leader as the culture editor and highlighted all the wrong things in Joseph's life. At roughly the same age, the man had become something. He wrote about music and films and had a girlfriend, or at least was "in a relationship," according to his MySpace page. But Joseph found himself thanking the newspaper writer, if inwardly, after finding Claire from Bornhoft's list of friends. Attractive, yes, but he also liked how she said she loved indie music, weird movies, and photography. Joseph's first message was cocky but self-deprecating, and sure enough it garnered a response. After a few texts, some of the first Joseph ever sent, including a long back-and-forth about P. T. Anderson films, then a six-hour talk on the phone, they arranged a date in Brookings, where she was a senior at South Dakota State University.

Before the night Joseph Bethel went to see Claire Hardy, chances had come and chances had gone. At this age, Joseph thought as he got ready, he should have been with someone. Trying to ditch the scruples gathered up during his twenty-four years on earth, Joseph drove north on I-29 to Claire's apartment. To the same apartment building, it turned out, as the one Joseph's sister lived in when she was in college. Going up the familiar stairs with the stained carpet, beer cans in the hall, Joseph began to sense an almost crippling nervousness. He could barely compose himself enough to knock. But he did, and she answered.

"Why hello," Claire said, opening the door, and, like they'd known each other for years, reached out into the hallway for a brusque embrace. Her voice had a gravelly roughness, but after they parted Joseph saw her pictures did not do her justice. Claire's thickness was new and intoxicating, her thighs and arms filled out her jeans and rock-band tee. The memory of her body made Joseph woozy as he took a step from the musky hallway into her incense-laden place.

"Come on in, ya handsome kid."

"Thanks," he said, beginning to scan her apartment. It had just the right blend of disarray and woman. "I guess we're both really good-looking and should just start making out." Joseph looked at Claire, and to his horror her face was a stone. Seconds ticked by, and at last she burst out with a big laugh. She took his coat and called him a "weirdo," their stale introduction blasted away by her confidence.

"Sit down, sit down," she said. "Did you want some coffee?" Joseph didn't drink coffee, but he said yes, not making a fuss when he smelled liquor in it, his first taste since that night with Sandra. They decided on a movie, *Reality Bites*, and as Claire, on her knees, searched in a stack of VHS tapes, Joseph marveled at her backside, how terrifically it popped out from her upper thighs, which were like the sturdy trunks of a tree. She came to the couch. Like nothing, she slid her legs onto his lap.

"That feels good," she said as Joseph began to rub her feet and the movie started. "Your hands are warm."

"My mom always said that, actually."

Claire laughed. "Yeah right, your mom."

Joseph had never given a foot rub to anyone other than his mom, and he changed the topic as best he could. "You have nice feet."

"You think? They're kinda big and gross, I always thought."

"No no, they're nice," Joseph said, and that's when Claire had to know. She'd not gotten herself involved with the worldly guy on the phone who could make her laugh, but someone dreadfully inexperienced, maybe even inept.

She put her head back down and closed her eyes. Joseph watched, wondering why Ben Stiller's character got such a raw deal. His sisters told him, One day you'll get it, but it didn't make any sense still. Soon enough, the credits rolled.

"So," Claire said. Her hair pointed in several directions. She had fallen asleep. "Did you want to just stay here?"

"For sure," Joseph said, trying to be cool, "sure."

Claire got up and left Joseph on the plushy couch. Not until he heard her begin to brush her teeth did he get up. In the bathroom, Claire's face clean and scrubbed, Joseph asked for gum. That's all he could think of.

"I don't think I have any," Claire mumbled, spitting out frothy water. "You can use my toothbrush if you want."

"No, no," he said. "I should be okay." Removing himself from the doorway, Joseph left Claire to get ready for bed and went to the kitchen. He poured himself a glass of water there, and, as he drank it down, he said softly but intensely, "Don't be such a freaking idiot." Like moving toward hell, he went to her bedroom.

Claire with the lights on, taking off her shirt. Her belly button pierced. It looked so good Joseph had to look away at the liner notes of a CD on her bureau. He did not know what else to do. Just as soon as he looked back, he saw she had lost her jeans. It was so much, Joseph experienced at that moment a great loss, fearing he might never see something so perfect again. Claire crawled into bed, tucking herself under her downy white comforter, and Joseph got to work taking off his clothes. Once upon a time in college he went through the trouble of shaving off his chest hair, but, since no one ever saw him naked, he figured such a process was a waste, certainly not worth an itchy chest. Perhaps, he thought by Claire's bed, it might be time to start up again. He unzipped his jeans, wishing she would watch, but she was burrowed. Joseph climbed in. The lights off, neither said a word.

"Do you want a back rub?" he asked, sensing her heat but not feeling it. "I give a pretty good one."

"Oh, no, thank you, that's all right. I've got a test in the morning. I should get to sleep. Good night." And Claire curled to her side more.

Something had gone wrong, Joseph knew. Maybe it had been wrong the second he knocked on her door. The experience, which would not be happening that night, had once seemed so special but in fact it was a heavy burden. Claire's warm body near him, Joseph began to think of a universe where he had not prayed the prayer, a place where the ones he met in passing he also moved to orgasmic rapture: Megan's agape mouth, Victoria's shaking body, Sofia's swollen clitoris (something he'd read happened), Lily rocking up and down,

April's cheek rubbing against a headboard, Ashley's bosom all free.

Claire's breathing, steady and rhythmic, and the dream stopped. For an hour or two Joseph lay awake, and for weeks after he wished that night away, thinking only of Mary.

8

Claire never returned any of the phone calls Joseph made over the next week, which confirmed, for him, that a serious mistake had been made. Joseph wanted to know what it was, so as to avoid it in the future, but he didn't try calling a fourth time. It was unlike him to let someone like Claire drift away, seeing as he pined after Mary for nearly two years, but Joseph had to admit to himself that Claire Hardy would never, not in this world, be his wife. So in that knowledge he felt relieved, or at least not heartbroken. Though maybe the real reason Joseph never dwelled on Claire is because another appeared, expediting the recovery process. Suzanne Tucker lived in Birmingham, Alabama, and there was Joseph in Sioux Falls in his studio apartment, appreciating long bounds of auburn hair, and a forehead, glistening from the summer heat, then beyond that, the black night sky. This woman did not look in the camera; instead her eyes were set out and above. Again she came from MySpace, and a few days after messaging her, Joseph had a reply.

> You're not one of those internet playas are you? I am on to you Joey Jo. Have a great day. Bye-bye now. Suzanne

Being called "Joey Jo" for the rest of his life didn't seem so bad. Joseph responded right away, but Suzanne didn't write back for a week, and when she did it was a short, impersonal message about how she had no plans of seeing anyone for a while. It neared Thanksgiving, and as Joseph read her note, he thought about the Christmas before, of the night he held Mary's hand. It happened only once. Not even a sliver of that confidence remained. But there must be magic in disinterest, as Suzanne sent a message a week later, offering her phone number by embedding the numbers within the body of the email. The same night, an hour into their first talk, Joseph learned Suzanne had been born again a year and a half earlier. Before that, she said, she smoked "a lot of pot" and lived with her boyfriend.

"It's not what God wants anymore," Suzanne told Joseph. Her voice was honey. "I'm looking for a man that's gonna be the spiritual leader in the relationship."

"Of course," Joseph said from his boxy apartment. Posters of movies—*Fargo* and *Punch-Drunk Love*—hung on white walls. It was winter.

"I want a man that's gonna lead me spiritually, and when I meet him he'll be at a place, spiritually, much further than I am. He'll bring me along. You understand, right, Joey Jo?"

"The man has to be the leader, I agree. I've been through a lot, Suzanne. I've grown. And like I told you, I haven't had sex, but I have to be honest, that's kind of embarrassing at this point."

"No no, Joey, that's the sweetest thing. It shows how faithful you've been. It's rare to find a guy who holds sex so sacred. It's beautiful."

"Really?"

"Yes, Joey, yes. I can't tell you how many guys I've met, even Christian guys, who think it's just some thing they gotta get out of the way before they meet their wife. I love that you've kept your body holy. I really do."

"The older I get, the weirder it is to tell girls that. I do hope I meet her soon."

"Oh sweet Joey, I'm so sure you're gonna meet her real soon. God will provide her and she's gonna be more amazing than you ever thought."

"I hope so."

"Don't hope, Joey, know. Know you're a catch. I mean that. The girl you marry is gonna be so lucky."

Like that it went for hours, and there were times when Suzanne would take pains to not mislead Joseph into believing she would be on the other end of that catch, though their phone sex did confuse things. One evening, not long into their courtship, Suzanne explained what she wore to bed—a pair of see-through black panties and no top—while Joseph said he wore red boxer-briefs. That night he drank vodka, diluting it with ice cubes and healthy pours of orange juice. "It'd be nice," she had said, "for your first drunk experience to be with me."

"Sooo," Joseph was saying. "I am definitely drunk."

"Oh I like that, Joey. Tell me something sexy."

"Okay. What are you wearing?"

"Panties, my black see-through ones."

"That's so cool. I'm sorry if I'm not making sense. I think I might be drunk." And he sang it like "I Think I Need a New Heart" from his favorite secular album, *69 Love Songs.* "I think I might be druuunnnnnk."

"Keep going," Suzanne said.

"So, okay, if I was there with you, I'd take your hands in mine, then I'd slowly brush my fingers up your arms and across your shoulders and down your beautiful back."

"That's nice, Joey."

"And I'd blow on your neck, working my way down your body."

"Mmhmm."

"I'd brush my cheek against yours and kiss you softly, then a little more so you can feel me."

"That's nice, Joey, really nice. Are you hard?"

"I got it out. It's pretty hard."

"I'm so wet." And Suzanne moaned. Joseph could hardly believe it. This was as special to him as hearing the first transmission of life in space would be for an astronaut.

"I'm stroking it," Joseph said, unsure of the words coming out of his mouth.

"Wait a second, Joey, I'm gonna get something." In the silence, Joseph tried to collect his thoughts, though it proved difficult while masturbating. "I hope you don't mind," Suzanne said when she got back. A buzzing started, and they headed to a climax.

In the cold, vacant moments afterward, the phone on his cheek, a slimy residue on his stomach, Joseph thought he heard crying. He put the phone closer to his ear.

"I'm so sorry," Suzanne was saying. "I'm sooo sorry."

"Suzanne, what, no, I'm sorry." But Joseph was in no position to console anyone, drunk and a thousand miles away.

"It's just." Suzanne sniffed. "I jus' don't think we should be doing these kinds of things, not until we're married. I know. You know. We both know God can use us in better ways."

"Right," Joseph said. "Right," he repeated, even if they did the same thing every few nights, the space in between full of prayer, until that waned and their desire overtook them again.

About a month later Joseph Bethel arrived to a balmy Alabama in December, finding Suzanne near the baggage line. The experience of meeting her would not be like meeting Mary, mind-blowing in a celestial sense, but Suzanne was attractive, if not even more so than Mary. She wore no makeup and had good, feminine fat. She was firm and tight in important places. They hugged hello and she emanated garden waves, like flowery herbs. Joseph wanted that scent always in his life.

"So what do you think?" he asked after they separated. Suzanne had been anxious about appearance. "Do I look better or worse than the pictures?"

"Handsome boy. Very handsome indeed." They had another hug, then they walked out of the airport hand in hand.

In her apartment in an affluent, almost entirely white neighborhood of Birmingham, they took a few minutes to eat fresh fruit she had prepared in a wicker basket. After that, like most of the trip, they were on top of each other and exploring.

As breaks from the physical, they went to her church and met her friends, ate formal dinners with her family. The rest of the time, nakedness. On the night before Joseph was to leave, they were in her bedroom, like a large casket underneath her living room—getting there through a trap door in her single-room apartment—and Suzanne ran her fingers through his hair. How great marriage would be, Joseph thought. Lying in bed, a Southern sculptor who once smoked a lot of weed but now runs an organic grocery store is running her fingers through your hair.

"That wouldn't be a big deal," Joseph was saying, "I could get a job part-time, couldn't I? Start a business or something. That'd be perfect."

"More than perfect," Suzanne said and took Joseph in her right hand, placing it against her warmth. It was the best substitute, said had told him, for sex, the closest to feeling the experience without actually experiencing the feeling. As the sun rose, Joseph moved his hand sleepily down her stomach, and that's when it happened.

"Fuck me," Suzanne said, pushing away his hand. "I wanna be fucked, please."

"I thought…"

"Don't talk, Joseph. Just fuck me, please." Joseph was limp, so Suzanne crawled over and took him in her mouth. "Most girls don't like it, but I love it," she had said proudly on their first night. Suzanne spit it out. "You're going to love this, Joseph," she whispered as she situated herself on him, so close her breasts were like a preserver around his neck.

"I love you, Suzanne," he said as it started. "I really do." At last it was happening for Joseph Bethel, and he had to say, after they finished, he lasted longer than he'd thought he would.

Suzanne drove him to the airport later that day and Joseph couldn't help but keep glancing over at her with a goofy grin. God had provided. Someday, he thought, he would feel for her as much as he had for Mary. All the happiness, he would have it, that Joseph was sure of on the plane. A good marriage, living in Alabama with an artist, all the years of toiling and yearning coming to an end.

In Sioux Falls, snow blanketed the flat ground, and everything was big and out of place. The dark night of South Dakota contrasted with the temperate conditions of the South. The stewardess said it was okay to turn on cellular devices. Flipping open his phone, a message from Suzanne.

"On my way to prayer group," she said in the voice mail. "I wanted to thank you for the nice time."

Car sounds muffled her, so Joseph couldn't be sure what she was trying to say. Maybe something happened at church. Suzanne mentioned a controversy with the worship leader, and it was late. Everything would make sense in the morning.

As soon as Joseph got up, he checked his phone. A text message. It hit him so hard, he read from his knees.

> 2 Corinth 6:14–7:1. I'm so sorry but when you
> left God showed me what I didn't want to see.
> He showed me my ways. I need to come back

to Him. I don't want to mess around, not at my age, not anymore. I know this must be hard for you to hear. But know this is from God. We can't see each other again. Please read the above passage and pray on it. I know I have.

A year later, Joseph lived in a new place. He'd found the upper level of a house with hardwood floors and plenty of space for five hundred dollars a month, utilities and cable included. In the afternoon, after another overnight at the children's home, he opened his eyes and stared at the ceiling. He heard the ambient sounds of the house. Outside his bedroom window, the streets were slumberous. January's winter, colder than the last, and barely a trace of snow sat on the ground. Putting his head back down, he thought of Mary, as he often did when coming in or out of sleep. It had been almost two years, and her face was less distinct. It once was a heavy weight. It used to be he could hardly move without thinking of what steps she was taking at that moment in Iowa. More and more he was trying to consider her fading memory a blessing, rather than a curse. Joseph got up out of bed. There was life to live.

9

If he could do it all over, if it could all be done again. This time, go back to the high school reunion, maybe his tenth, and get that good feeling. A woman on his arm, no longer a Mary or Suzanne, she has changed. Tattooed, she teaches yoga and takes pictures of herself in contorted positions then posts them to social media. In the old gym, under a homemade banner with an emblazoned "Class of '98," Joseph gives her a playful squeeze on the meaty part of her backside, pats the old quarterback, Brady, squarely on the shoulder, and says, "Sure is good to see you again. What did you say you were doing? Still working in town?"

Joseph Bethel's guide to that path has a name, and is from a place, and they met not long after he moved to the Pacific Northwest. She had curly hair and grew up in northern Minnesota. Another started the construction for all good roads to walk upon. Laurel King grew up just outside Portland,

Oregon, in an intentional Christian community—not that un-like Hutterites—and when she climaxed, Joseph learned not long after meeting her, she shuddered like a dying animal. It was a viscerally positive response to his fumbling attempts at satisfying the second woman he had ever been with, and he was very thankful for it. Though before he even felt the con-tractions, he was just glad to make her acquaintance by way of the church both his new roommates and Laurel attended.

In just his second week in the city he drove to Laurel's after making something up about the strings of his guitar—which he barely ever played—being broken. He went down I-5, driv-ing on the bridge that spanned the lake, then through the downtown tunnel, out to the southern part of the city where Mount Rainier takes up the skyline on clear days. Laurel lived in a poor but slowly gentrifying area, and as Joseph emerged from his white sedan—guitar in one hand—then trekked up hilly stairs that cut through a garden to her front door, he wondered how Laurel could be unattached. Did the new, "emerging" brand of Christianity allow for a little more fudge room when it came to the verses in the New Testament on lust and giving in to pleasure? It seemed impossible to Joseph for Laurel to not have a man, even as he rang the bell. In the front window, a sign promoted peace.

"Coming," Joseph heard in a lilting, feminine way. The door opened. "Hey, come on in." It was not Laurel, but anoth-er, in an outfit one might wear when working construction: a flannel top and outdoorsy, burnt-orange pants. Joseph watched her hips sway as she walked to a rocking chair. Picking up a curved knife from the windowsill, she began to whittle wood.

In the next space of time, Laurel came in with a hug. Then another appeared, a blonde with a happy hello. Three of them on the couch, they went around pretending to know how to fix the guitar, and all the while the one in the burnt-orange pants in the rocking chair kept whittling, letting the shavings fall into a cardboard box. Joseph had come a long way since laser tag, and all sensitive little boys must one day experience a great awakening when they find their right place in the world. This was it. It had to be.

No one knew how to fix the guitar, so Joseph put it back in its nylon case and relaxed as he drank a locally brewed beer. They moved to the evening's friendly rhythm. Crystal, the blonde, just out of college, was in Seattle to work with the poor. She told a story about how the house had put up an ad on the internet looking for friends, men mostly. She spoke in a soft voice.

"And this one guy sent us a picture, we think it was his senior picture. It was him leaning on his car, and without his shirt."

"Tell him about peanut butter guy," Tina added. The dry wood took more shape in her hands.

"Peanut butter guy," Joseph said. "Yeah, tell me about that guy. Sounds like a hunk."

"I could," Crystal said with an evil smile. "Or, I could talk about the one who wanted just your number, Tina."

Tina, turning red, mumbled a deflecting "whatever" and pretended to concentrate on her project. Joseph spoke up for her. "I don't know, Tina, whoever he is, it sounds like you missed out on your real shot with peanut butter guy." All three of the women giggled. How thankful Joseph felt to hear that chorus.

It turned to evening and Joseph had told more jokes, the ones stored up in his years of living alone. When it became bedtime, Tina and Crystal went to their rooms, leaving Laurel and Joseph to themselves. The dim light and cozy blankets drew them close.

"I'm not tired," Laurel said. Hers was the kind of body that could teach yoga, though she did not have tattoos. "I should be, but I'm not. Work, who cares." And she touched her hair, mentioning that she needed to have it cut. This alone steered them off to where they both wanted to go.

"I like the red hair," Joseph said.

"Oh, thank you, but it's more like auburn, see?" Laurel tilted her head. Feelings, just feeling feelings, could be allowed now. Joseph took a cord of her hair, and Laurel moved closer, close enough that he began crawling his hands up the back of her neck with the tips of his fingers.

"Do you give head rubs?" Laurel asked, anticipating.

The hairs on Joseph's arms and legs stood up, and as if he had been doing this kind of thing since puberty, he said, "I'm surprised you haven't heard about my skills, Laurel."

They situated themselves. Laurel's butt pressed against his crotch, and as Joseph Bethel began kneading Laurel King's skull, the rest of the house snored. A small but encouraging noise, like a release, and Joseph moved in closer, noticing the smell of her shampoo. She turned. Their lips met. The couch enveloped them.

The next night was a party at Joseph's new shared house, one someone before he moved there had dubbed "Substance." It had been advertised to him as a commune, of sorts, in a region between Ballard and Fremont. The people there had a name for the neighborhood, but Joseph never mentioned it to his parents. He knew Dad would repeat it tirelessly as a joke, until it became unspeakable. The area suited Joseph fine. Close to a giant grocery-slash-department store, it reminded him of home. Near bus lines, so one could get to other, more sophisticated parts of the city quickly, if need be.

All the noises from the party spilled out into Joseph's new neighborhood, the talks on Nietzsche and Chesterton. Everyone in Substance that night attended a church called Church of the Wanderers, where they used words like "relationality" in earnest. They found it after their youthful faith reached its logical end. Its congregants curated many parties, and at that first one Joseph was still hoping "she" might come, that The One might be there. By then, more evolved in her view of God, she would arrive in tastefully revealing clothing.

In slinky skirts over black tights, colorful headbands pulling back their long hair, they huddled in the kitchen, standing like twinkling ornaments on the brown-stained tile. The rest, those who used words like "frak" instead of "fuck," milled about in the living room. Joseph was there, longing for the kitchen. Just then, Darla Jones, one of his roommates at Substance, raised her glass. A birthmark covered most of her face.

"It's fine," one of the others said, pulling Darla's hand down. "It's not a big deal." Darla wrenched her hand out of the grip, causing red wine to spill on the wood floor.

"I just get so fucking sick of it," Darla said. The wine appeared black. "I get so fucking sick of doing all the work. And everyone else just fucking expects everything to get done. Just fucking expects it."

She spoke loudly enough on the church's politics for those in the kitchen to hear, but they did not seem to care. Someone in the living room went and got towels to clean the spill, and because Darla was too drunk to really help soak up the mess, she punched at it with one hand, holding her wine in the other. In the kitchen, Joseph was eyeing the kind of woman every God-fearing man with vaguely artistic aspirations could ever want: full-bodied, with wavy hair, and tattooed. He got up and went close enough to touch the hem of her fashionable top. The woman, maybe a girl, probably not yet twenty-two, held her wine glass aristocratically, dipping crackers into a plate of hummus. Nursing his drink, Joseph wanted to say some-thing, maybe about a Renaissance painting, or how the last Radiohead album was perfect to listen to during Eucharist, or about the latest ecumenical book by Rob Bell.

Moments went by. Nothing came, like there was someone catching his throat. Joseph pretended to cough and shuffled in another direction, closer to another by the refrigerator. She wore a puffy shirt, billowing white ruffles up to her neck like the plumage of a jungle bird. Her face was pristine and her body was maybe more than Joseph could handle, but he want-ed to try. Getting up with a beer from the fridge, she began talking with a woman next to her with silken hair cut in a thick bowl. Joseph's roommates had said that girl knew "more than anybody" about movies, which had given him a pang. For a brief time in Sioux Falls Joseph thought he could be a movie critic. That dream was gone, along with the one after that, of becoming a stand-up comedian. If he could just say something about The Decalogue, that might impress the one with the bowl cut, and she would tell the one with the pristine face how this new guy who lived in Substance knew about interesting things.

At that time, just after moving to Seattle, Joseph was in the best shape of his life. He had all his hair, even if worries of losing it plagued him. As that man, he approached, but an interruption stopped everything. The kitchen turned its collective head. Someone was standing on a chair. It was Jerry, the head deacon at Church of the Wanderers, known to everyone at the party. He cleared his throat again. The ones in the living room squeezed through the doorway, like baby birds elongating their necks for a meal.

"We're doing it," Jerry said. "It's happening." And the room erupted in applause.

As Joseph would later learn, Jerry and his wife, Carrie—the worship music leader at Church of the Wanderers—had long planned to travel to Africa to start a charity. Jerry's bone-thin wife stood by her husband, her hair cut in a mullet. She wore something that, Joseph thought, she'd stitched that afternoon.

"We'll both be leaving our jobs," Carrie picked up. "But we won't be selling the house, so we'll be looking for anyone who wants a place to house-sit." And she smiled mirthfully at everyone.

They would have offers, Joseph was sure of that, as he moved away from those queuing up to congratulate the couple, to the living room, where a Sufjan Stevens album played. Darla was seated on the couch drinking. Around them religious iconography was arranged on the mantel above the fireplace, framed pictures of starving Africans and Belltown crack addicts. The rest of the losers—though no one in the kitchen made such distinctions—soon came back and settled in their places. Jerry came with them, changing the music over to a mix he'd brought himself. The same beat played over and over.

"I wouldn't wanna miss out on cards," Jerry said, reaching in his tweed suit coat pocket to pull out a flask. Noises from the kitchen, of people laughing. It was the two Joseph wanted to talk with; they were standing so close. Stars combust like that, Joseph thought.

Jerry took a drink, grimacing after he swallowed, then looked out the picture window of the house. Perhaps, Joseph thought sarcastically, for a soul as deep as his. Then Joseph's other roommate at Substance, a civil engineer who always wore a multicultural wrap around her head, fell from her chair but somehow managed to hold on to her drink. Her fall flipped up her skirt and the whole table laughed. The party was devolving.

"On second thought," another said. "I should get going." And like that, she got up.

Some of the partiers went to watch their sister scoot away down the street. Joseph did too, and was glad then to see Laurel, and her auburn hair, coming up the sidewalk. She wore a black coat over a small black dress and she strode into the windowed entry. They hugged, an embrace saying a hard day's work was done. Laurel filled the small space with the aroma of a social evening, a mixture of perfumes and baked food and cigarette smoke. She'd worked that night at an auction to benefit the homeless, one where citizens from neighborhoods like Queen Anne and the bluffs above the arboretum and the lavish mansions on Capitol Hill bought things like trips to the San Juan Islands to help end poverty.

Through the living room holding hands, they received scattered hellos. For almost ten years before that moment Joseph had worked out his salvation, but he did not think of God then, only that every step he took brought him closer to a bedroom, and everyone at the party knew that. The shared knowledge brought him the greatest pride he'd known since qualifying for state in high school golf, years before. Even as they went by the one with the pristine face and the one who ate hummus delicately, Joseph's steps remained sure. Laurel was prettier than most, and she did not need God to tell her that. It gave her an air of danger the other two could only dream of. They got to his room.

"So, this is it," Joseph said as he closed the door. White Christmas lights strung above gave a magical air. There was no bed yet, only blankets and egg foam, but there was a television. They lay down and started to watch a documentary about a religious camp in North Dakota. The viewing did not last long, and whatever Joseph did, however clumsily it was done, made Laurel seize up and shake.

How greatly did the escape to Seattle assure him. So great, Joseph could not begin to think that one day he would live every moment of his life wishing he could start all over again. It was the furthest thing from his mind, but trouble was moving fast.

10

They amassed quality moments. Watching independent films, eating Vietnamese soup, they accumulated their share of intimacies. On a Friday evening, Joseph drove again to Laurel, on the interstate cutting through the heart of the city. A song played at such a high volume in his car it shook the rear-view mirror. Joseph envisioned himself powerful, like a rock star in front of thousands of people. Driving and not caring if his tires flew off his car.

Near her place, at the corner of Othello and Rainier, Joseph stopped for a candy bar and something to quench his thirst. After biting down on the chocolate, he recognized, with a great swallow of soda, that he had become a man. The weather was clear, unusual for late winter in Seattle, and the sun just beginning to set. He thought positive thoughts. There had been rumors from Laurel of Tina recently pairing with Lars, a guy who worked building houses with her, and turning down the women's narrow street, Joseph began to understand, as he had been understanding more in Seattle—finding himself at ease enough to make general observations about the nature of the world—that it was actually not God who granted favor, but that some guys like Tony and Lars were just lucky. If a Creator did exist, Joseph theorized, He did not have a plan for each and every soul wandering the earth.

Jealousy dissipated more quickly than in the past. Joseph could, instead of feeling sorry for himself for being alone, rest easy knowing that Laurel, with the auburn hair and the yoga body, would be with him at night. She would lay her head on his chest and give him warmth as they drifted off to sleep. Everyone at the house of women knew what Joseph and Laurel did, but they all seemed to think of it like, "They're just two new friends having fun." How liberal the new world was.

The road Joseph drove on went down steeply, reaching to the bottom of the valley and Martin Luther King Boulevard. About halfway down, Joseph parked beside the house where Laurel and the women lived, deciding, like he'd decided before, to park as close as he could, his car facing the oncoming traffic. Parking in either direction was just fine in Seattle.

But that's when the thoughts came, the ones planted at birth and watered in a dorm room with a girl named Sandra, and growing with years spent alone. These thoughts had worsened in Sioux Falls. There, after masturbating in his studio apartment, they traveled through his body to say, "Get everything clean. If you don't, all the sin germs might one day infect the next person who lives here, so you need to clean the steps from the computer to the shower and wash the towels used to dry your body after and don't touch anything while doing it or else start the whole process over again for fear of something terrible happening to anyone unlucky enough to have been thought about while cleaning."

They continued as Joseph drove to Seattle from Sioux Falls. On more than one occasion they convinced him he was running over things in the road and ruining the lives of those he would never know. Joseph turned off his car by the house of women. As he put the keys in his hand, the thoughts started up again.

"You parked too close to the car in front of you." Above him was Laurel. She would be fit and smart and everything he wanted. "What if someone parks close to you? They might have a tough time getting out. They'll bump your car. Worse, the car behind them, they'll hit it and get into an accident and they don't have insurance. Their life is ruined."

Joseph took steps away, telling himself he was insane, but they followed him up the sidewalk, cutting back and forth like switchbacks. They shouted, loudly enough that his movement up the concrete stairs became tentative. An avalanche of boulders toppled in front of him, so he turned. Back at the car, playing with his door handle, Joseph saw the road above, straight and flat.

"Just get it over with," he said out loud. Getting in roughly, like a trucker, Joseph drove down to a driveway. He took a right and put the car in reverse, and in that neighborhood of Seattle, on that street, the cars connected like a chain of train cars. In Sioux Falls, every family had their own driveway, so Joseph backed up, and the next sound was of crunching plastics and metals.

It should be noted, most others would've had the common sense to call the insurance company or the cops. Or, if they were particularly hard, just left it, saying to themselves, "It ain't that big of a deal, this guy's probably got insurance." But Joseph viewed what had just happened as an intractable nightmare. In the shadows he examined the dent closely, trailing his fingers softly over the bruise on the truck's side door. With no pen or paper, he got back in his car, carefully this time, and drove up the hill and parked. That very day he'd switched insurance companies. Would the new one work? Would the old one? For a second Joseph thought of calling his dad. But he just couldn't do it, not in his new world of courageous autonomy. So Joseph held it in and walked to the women in the house.

"Heeey," Tina greeted him. She was knitting in the lamp-lit living room. The room smelled of cooked vegetables. Joseph said hello and walked straight to the kitchen to get a piece of paper and pen. With those things, he went back through.

"Hey," Laurel said this time. "Leaving so soon?"

"Be right back. Forgot something," Joseph said, and Laurel smiled at him as he went out the door.

In the silence of his sedan, Joseph wrote the most comprehensive note he could manage, putting down his information, address and name and phone number, then he clipped the note under the wiper of the truck, and thought again, for a moment, of calling his dad, but once more did not. After that Joseph went inside, sat next to Laurel going over their days, though he added very little to the conversation. Because on his scalp, he could feel it, the punishment once reserved for when he gave in to base temptations, God pulling out each one of his hairs, one by one by one.

11

Whenever fate decides, Joseph Bethel will once more gather the scraps Bethany Fergus left behind—a Polaroid, two emails, the fading memories of her body—and get more depressed than sentimental, remembering a scratch in history where she would have considered him seriously as a mate. Even on his best days now, Joseph knows he would not be good enough for Bethany. They have not seen each other in years, but she is still perfect, frozen in unending nostalgia.

She had just eclipsed her teenage years when they met, so Bethany would have been under the drinking age at the kickball party that young spring at the house of women. Whether legal or not, she drank a beer with the rest of them. As though winning an amazing raffle, Joseph watched as she and the rest tumbled through the front door of Laurel's house, like coming out of—or maybe entering into—a clown car crammed full of fresh-faced, photogenic young people. They carried with them the dreams of expectant parents, yet the only thing these children seemed to want to do was be young, drink IPAs and see one another naked. Lost in it, Joseph sipped from a bottle with a bike on the label. How unique and appealing it was to watch bearded men and their sensual counterparts, with paint-splattered jeans and unshaved armpits. Pausing after another drink, the commotion became a pleasant score as he thumbed through photos. One of them was always on Laurel's dinner table, or on the kitchen windowsill, or some other place in the house, and often it got passed around and inspected. In the photo, all the house builders smile in two rows, arranged to commemorate a day at a construction site. The wind appears to howl, and in the front, all the way to the right, one of the workers buries her hands deep in her flannel pockets. She wears tough work clothes and a stocking hat, out of which sprout curls. At that moment, a burst of laughter, and Joseph smiled inwardly because it was charming. He liked when he heard it, more than any other laugh at the party. Getting up, he went to the kitchen where Laurel stirred vegetables in a wok.

"Just go back there," she said. "They won't bite."

"But don't you need help?" Joseph asked as he stole a morsel of food, then gulped out the words, "I'm a really good kitchen helper."

"I'm sure. Just go," she said, and wiped off his kiss with her shoulder.

In the backyard, a patch of grass, a clothesline, a wooden fence and a pea patch. A few burly men talked to each other about a truss recently blown over at their site. Just down the street was the pickup.

"Drive your car over a bridge," a voice rang out.

Taking a hard swig, Joseph nodded at no one and went back inside. In the living room, Lars, Tina's man at the time, blond and wearing a red and green plaid shirt, told the story of how he and the curly-haired one from the picture came out to Seattle together. Tofu burgers and kale chips devoured as they listened, along with chips dipped in organic salsas; they drank hoppy beer too.

"We met in the library," Lars said, and just by standing in that library he must have looked like someone saving the world, his wild blond hair and stocking hat slightly tipped back. "I think we were the only two people at Concordia with longboards."

"We both wanted to get out," the curly-haired one added. Her name was Bethany. "Seattle seemed like the place to go."

Later, while on the stereo a pop singer whistled about palindromes, Bethany began to pick at the strings of a guitar. It seemed nothing would happen at first, but then the whistling singer was turned down and Lars shouted, "Let's hear it, Beth!"

"Mrr," she said. "I don't know. My calluses are all gone." And she lifted her hands to show but strummed some chords anyway. She played a whole song Joseph had never heard before but would, years later, never want to hear again. When she finished, Joseph's claps were the loudest.

The party, hours later. Another had become the center of attention on the same couch where Joseph first rubbed Laurel's head. His name was Moonshadow, as he knew every Cat Stevens song, and with what remained of the party—after more dark beers—they sang along to each requested tune. Bethany had left. Laurel was there.

"Okay," Moonshadow said before the last one. "This has got to be it." He could play the guitar and sing well, and the women, Laurel too, seemed to love him. How easily that feeling transferred from one person to the next. Joseph knew that. It was the same day he fell for Bethany Fergus.

The next morning after kissing each other goodbye, Laurel turned on her Saturday morning NPR radio program and Joseph left to alleviate his mind. Upon arrival to the truck, he examined the windshield. The note was gone. Breathing in the fresh air, he dreaded, like a big test he forgot to study for, that the house in line with the truck would in fact be the wrong house and the man inside would have no idea what the person in front of him went on about.

"A note? On where?"

Joseph almost turned around to go home to Substance, knowing he had little money to give. But the thoughts began again. "You fuck. Be a man and get it over with." There was no choice.

The doorbell made a loud dong. A dog began barking. The clicking of paws against a wood floor. It lunged toward Joseph, hoarsely guarding whatever it believed it needed to guard. Joseph rang the bell again, but this time there was the pushing of furniture and the shuffling of feet, the creaking of floorboards. The slick-furred dog kept barking at the door, now opened just a crack.

"Hello," Joseph said through the slit. "Sorry to bother you, sir. But, if you had a minute, I had a question."

"Ronny, shut up!" the man fiercely commanded the dog, then casually looked at Joseph. "Go ahead, son."

"Sorry to bother you, but did you happen to own that pick-up, the tan one?" Joseph pointed. "I left a note on it."

"Yeah," the man said.

"You know the one I'm talking about? About me backing into you?"

"Yeah," the man said again and again yelled at the dog. The barking abated, for a second.

"I was afraid you didn't get it."

"No, man." The barking just got louder. "*Hush up*, Ronny!" The man slapped the dog on the nose.

"I'm sorry," Joseph said over the noise. "I just moved here and didn't know how easy it was to back into something."

"That's all right, man, you got insurance?"

"I do. But I actually changed companies, so I don't know how that will work."

"No problem. It's honest of you to come over like this. One time I had a guy drive down this road and rip half my front end off. Never left a note or nuthin'."

"Wow," Joseph said, thinking all of a sudden that they might start a friendship. Bond over reckless drivers and loud dogs. "Did you have my information and everything?"

"Sure," the man said. "But, let me tell you what, since you're new in town. I'll see how much my insurance covers and you just pay me the difference."

"Sounds great." And though Joseph did not know what paying the difference meant, he didn't care. A resolution was in sight. The weight of all problems became as light as a single grain of sand.

"Let me give you my information." The man went away and Joseph waited as the dog kept barking. When he came back, the man had written his name and number with a black Sharpie on a slip of orange construction paper.

"Here you go." The man passed the note through the crack.

"Thanks," Joseph said. "I'll wait to hear from you then?"

"All right, let's do that." The man went back in the house, and Joseph turned away. As the outer door swung shut, the sounds of the barking waned and a hot metallic anxiety melted away. Piney goodness filled the air. Joseph had no thoughts. Driving back to Substance, he juggled the stars and the sun and the moon.

12

If someone had asked, Joseph would've said he was happy. He started work at two jobs, one in the morning for a package delivery company, loading trucks, and another waxing yachts during the day. He made money while getting in the best shape of his life, he had most of his hair, and he continued to meet people, often without even trying. Everyone in his expanding circle exuded attractiveness, all of them doing things he'd always wanted to do before—pub trivia, karaoke, adult intramural sports—but could never seem to find the crew.

The only thing acting as an inhibitor to the new world where guilt and constant worry of sin no longer reigned was the living arrangement. Sometimes, living at Substance meant having to attend Church of the Wanderers events, and every Thursday evening it was more or less a requirement to take part in a weekly sharing time, which amounted to Joseph's roommates agonizing over unfair cliques within the church, but it paid to be pragmatic and fulfill the inescapable duty. Finding a cheap room with good roommates from a thousand miles was not something, if the cards had to be shuffled and dealt again, he would likely fall into.

One of those Thursday nights, instead of the usual group talk, the church, comprised of universal Episcopalians and ex-fundamental Christians, hosted a Seder meal. The meal would be officiated by Friar Travis, as they called him, an obese man who quoted Monty Python movies, swore like a sailor, and got drunk. Whether these things were sins or not, the church members did not seem to care. They believed themselves genuine, unlike their brothers at Mars Hill. Even if the Church of the Wanderer's finance campaigner attended the same conferences, they deemed themselves spiritually separate.

"Fold your hands, and receive the matzo," Friar Travis told the group of about twenty people at the Seder.

Sitting next to the friar's wife, a wisp of a woman, Joseph passed the bread and wine—in the right order or not, he had no idea—and hoped to avoid questions from her about his personal walk with God. But the friar's wife—and everyone else, including the two Joseph had lusted after at the first party—hardly looked his way, much less asked him about his innermost thoughts. Their nature, whether imagined as conceited or not, would be for Joseph one more reason to never return. And while walking back to Substance alone that night, Joseph considered his soul unfettered. In the glittering lights of evening, everything could be seen falling into place.

That weekend was another party, this time for Bob Dorling, who worked as a site manager where Tina and Bethany and the others built houses for the poor. Joseph had never seen Bob, only heard of the man and how he attracted not only Tina, but another who worked with them and also lived at the house with Laurel. Her name was Jennifer Loren. She and Tina shared their feelings for Bob, a bunk bed in Seattle, and before that, a dorm at a private Christian university in Iowa. Their fight for Bob's affection did not last long, coming to a head in Vancouver on a vacation paid for by the board of the house-building organization, in a hot tub of all places.

Tina would want a stable man like Bob, Joseph thought when he found out about the burgeoning relationship, not a lone wolf like Lars. Someone like Bob Dorling, with a job in construction, could take care of her. He could split wood in the winter, throw a Frisbee back and forth in the summer, stroll through Sunday markets in the fall. The rain on their rooftop in the spring as Tina knitted a new pair of long socks and he read a book of manly short stories. A guy like Lars, who got high and watched parkour videos on the internet then went ahead and jumped off urban structures in parks at all hours of the night, would be a guy for someone a little less serious. Bob was dependable and knew carpentry. He grew up in Ohio.

"So, we were in the hot tub," Tina told Joseph and Laurel at the women's house. "And we were both drunk, and one thing led to another, and we sort of started smooching." And that was pretty much the whole story, or at least all Tina was willing to tell. They were an item; what more was there to say?

How Tina and Bob began is what Joseph used as leverage in arguments with himself if, as he imagined, someone happened to ask why he was talking to Bethany if he already had Laurel. He could just say, "We're all adults, aren't we?"

Bethany would be at the German bar near the U-District for Bob's party. Joseph walked in and spotted Laurel with Headley, a man the women met through the same ad as the peanut butter guy. Standing around a raised table near the darts, he and Laurel drank beers out of boots.

"Mr. Joseph," Headley said, waving and ready to give a side hug at the same time. "I want you to meet my good friend. I don't think you two have met." He lifted a glass boot with two hands.

"Looks like a pretty good friend."

"Oh yes, Mr. Joseph." Headley smiled the kind of smile that could break out into a laugh at any moment. "Beer is the friend we have in Jesus."

Bob sidled up to the table with Tina then. The man had a handsome beard. Tina's hair was back in braids. They both wore flannels, their jeans muddied with caulk and dirt and paint.

"Happy Birthday," Joseph said, shaking Bob's hand.

"Let's play darts," was Bob's unceremonious reply.

So they did, and at some point after more drinks, people got lost. Who was with whom no longer mattered. Joseph and Bethany, in the middle of the bar. She wore work clothes, her curly hair in a bun; they discussed trivia from the week before. Headley was the quizmaster and had dedicated a category to Kevin Costner movies.

"How do you know about Morgan Freeman as Azeem?" Joseph looked behind, pretending to examine security at the front door. "Actually, better question, how did you get in here?" Someone had said Bethany was twenty years old.

"Don't you worry about that, buddy, and I know *Prince of Thieves*."

"Okay," Joseph countered. "But did you see it at your first sleepover at Brady Walter's house? You know Brady Walter, won the hundred-meter at state? Yeah, a sleepover at his house in the sixth grade, Bethany. Pretty special."

Bethany playfully slugged Joseph's shoulder. Her face shaded by the dark lighting of the bar, her presence filled his heart. The sounds of her voice blotted all others.

"Maybe we should watch it again?" she asked. "It's what Brady would want." And though Joseph hadn't asked, Bethany got a pen out of her purse—a cloth one with a heart stitched on its side—and wrote down her number. It burned on his hand like a tattoo.

For the next week Joseph called every day, only once getting Bethany's voice mail, though he liked it just as much, how sunny it was.

"Hi everyone, it's Bethany's phone, sorry I'm not here. Leave a message and I'll call you back. Byyye."

They went over the details of her upbringing in Minnesota and his in South Dakota. Sometimes it was hard to hear her, with Bethany's shared house along a busy street near Lake Union, so she'd go inside and tell Joseph about the organic bread she just baked, or a new song one of her roommates played on repeat. On the day they were to watch *Prince of Thieves*, Laurel asked Joseph about going to a brewery with Headley and others.

"I'll probably just relax today," was Joseph's answer. Before that conversation with Laurel, Joseph always believed he would be an honest man. When his options increased, it seemed, his morality did not.

Bethany and Joseph met at Gas Works Park. Rusted industrial equipment took up a portion of the grounds, machines that once powered the city. Bethany bounced out to the open field where Joseph waited with two gloves. She wore blue jeans and a shirt depicting an ocean. Later, he'd look back on that moment later as the first time he realized Bethany Fergus was perfect. They were alone, the weather classically dreary, throwing a softball back and forth. They tried a couple throws with the baseball.

"This is way better," Bethany said as she stepped backward with a softball, almost tripping as she did, letting out her goofy laugh. Joseph went even farther back. At that distance, the first time he threw the ball it skipped in front of, then by her.

"Sorry," he yelled, waving a glove in the air.

"That's okay," she said, waving back, running to it like a tomboy.

Joseph moved closer, close enough to see the details of Bethany's face. The day, to him, held innocence and hope and newness as they made a game of throwing higher and higher pop flies, and every time Joseph threw it in the sky, Bethany would say, "Oh boy, oh boy, oh boy," and catch the ball with her arm straight out. Though the only thing Joseph remembers of the day—even if it is not exactly what happened, just close enough to keep it this way in his memory—is Bethany lying on grass, looking up and laughing.

When they were done playing catch, they went to her place nearby. At dusk, she pulled beers from her shared fridge, and Joseph drank happily, even if he had not acquired a taste. Seven years separating them, Bethany was still more experienced. They relaxed on the couch, there in the kind of rental house with brown walls and shag carpet and all the furniture is from Goodwill. The movie started, and neither spoke. Setting her bottle down, Bethany put her cold hand near Joseph's. Her pinky wandered, so he took her hand. They kissed. The light of the streetlights, the sound of occasional cars driving by, is all there was. Joseph did not want for more.

13

Women, jobs, the life of a young man on the rise. Soon Joseph would move up at his package delivery company as well. Then, to finally relax. Worries of what one wants to be never to haunt him again. Instead, he could just be. No longer, Joseph imagined, would his family need to gloss over him when it came his turn to talk at family dinners. Even the worst anxiety, of finding a wife, had vanished. With so many choices in Seattle, it seemed absurd, the lamentation of years past. The one care Joseph did have would take care of itself. The man with the dog would call and say, "I've got the bill, son. It's about four hundred bucks. Ah, heck, since you were so honest, my insurance covered most of it, I'll just call it even."

A Friday night in that time, after Joseph worked his two jobs, he was back at Substance in his bedroom where he watched his team, the Minnesota Twins, play baseball—he'd bought a season pass on his computer. Another added bonus of the forged life was that working odd hours was over. He could be off with the rest of the world. How satisfying to be a normal man, relaxing at the right time of day. A text from Bethany came in on Joseph's flip phone.

"Going to bed," she wrote. "Gotta get up early and build those houses!"

"Yes," Joseph wrote back. "And the Twins are winning, Nick Punto just hit the ball! Amazing!" Whether she got the joke or not, it didn't matter, Bethany sent a smiley face emoticon in return.

Out in the living room, the crash of swords and loud gibberish. Joseph's roommates watched the *Lord of the Rings* movies in one sitting. A few innings went by in bliss and anticipation of sex. That heightened, a vacuuming sensation from his scrotum to his testicles, when he heard the sound of steps across the kitchen and toward his bedroom.

"Knock, knock," Laurel said as she pushed his door open. Inside, a candle burned, illuminating the cool dark. By then, Joseph had a bed, queen size, where Laurel put down her things. The white icicle lights hung above and framed posters of concerts on the wall: abstract dragons, elephants, and horned rams. A desk, wooden chair, dresser, and a stand housing his television, with a cheap DVD player and record player, and that was everything. The only space left in the middle is where Laurel undressed.

The next morning, Joseph looked over at his pale blue wall and thought of Bethany. Laurel snuggled into him.

"Breakfast?" she asked. They had been to breakfast at the place just down the street, the one owned by muscular lesbians, and to another nearby, run by disciples of the guru Sri Chinmoy. At each of them you waited an hour to get in. Joseph wanted to skip the bourgeoisie. He wanted cereal from a bag and maybe a donut or two. He also wanted Bethany.

"I don't know," he said. "I'm really not that hungry."

Laurel didn't press. She got out of bed and put on her clothes—nylon shirt and tights and cleats for biking—and Joseph got dressed too. No one else from Substance was up that sunny morning, so Joseph and Laurel stood alone between the driveway and the cement steps leading up to the house. Laurel pushed on her helmet and mounted her yellow bike. Joseph held her handlebars, sensing the end. That's the moment he managed to mumble out the suggestion that they have a talk.

"Joey," Laurel said. "I didn't think you ever wanted to have one of those. You don't seem the type." Which was not true at all, though Laurel had never known, and would never know, the Joseph who believed God preordained a woman from Iowa to work at a group home in Wyoming so she could meet a South Dakotan who would one day want nothing more than to ask her to be his wife.

"Right, maybe that's true," Joseph said, then, as bluntly as could be, "I'm not sure what you're thinking, but, y'know, I'm just not in a good place for a relationship."

Laurel winked, taking pity on the one who looked like he might start sweating. "We can work on just being friends, Joey, that'd be all right." It was as if Laurel had opened Joseph's skull and reached down into his brain and taken the words he wanted her to say.

"Okay, yeah," he said. "Definitely. That's good."

Laurel gave Joseph a kiss on the cheek, positioned her bike toward the road, and as he watched her bike away, it seemed less mournful than he had imagined it would be. Later that week, Laurel house-sat in Wallingford at a mansion with extra bathrooms and wood floors and chrome everything. She invited Joseph over and they drank free liquor and played video games on brand-new large televisions, and at the end of the night retired to one of the spare bedrooms. But that would be the last time, Joseph was sure of it, and as he drove away the next morning he told himself he would focus on Bethany. But then there was Alexis.

It started when they both volunteered at KEXP. Alexis was born and raised in California and spoke with an accent, "like, you know." Her sleek hair was cut short, and she wore brown-framed glasses, though what Joseph loved the most was her lips, fuller than anyone's he had seen or kissed. A night after house-sitting, Joseph went to Alexis's studio apartment. He had on his green boxer-briefs and Alexis wore nothing more than her black spandex yoga pants. On top of the covers, a movie played.

"Gawd," Alexis said as Joseph kneaded her back, "you are such a party pooper. Are you too cool to go?" A concert: Alexis wanted Joseph to see a live band with her. It was a constant struggle between them, Joseph wanting to stay in and fool around and Alexis wanting to go out and get drunk.

"I'm too old," Joseph said, since he considered himself a good ten years older than he was.

"Oh my God, Joseph, you're ridiculous, don't you want to see all this music? I'm sure North Dakota or whatever never had bands like this."

Joseph had to admit, even in South Dakota, they did not, though as many shows as Alexis suggested, Joseph suggested movies even more, the ones she "had to see." That night, they watched *Persona*. Joseph sat on her backside and commentated while she lay with her face down on the bed.

"So there's a woman and it's black and white, and she's kind of like looking through a camera. Okay, now there's this twin doing something else."

Joseph went lower, past a tattoo of a butterfly stretching from shoulder blade to shoulder blade. It was rugged, as if done in jail, though Alexis never commented on regretting it. She was the type who would have a butterfly tattoo on her upper back and not apologize for it. When his hands tired, Joseph lay beside her, and they began to wrestle. She lost her yoga pants. He kissed her forehead, her cheeks, her lips, and for a second, Alexis, a biochemist, once engaged, kissed Joseph in return. But then, and this—or some variation to distract—happened almost every time they did this, she bit down hard on his bottom lip.

"You're silly," she said, and Joseph rolled off, his eyes watering. "Come come, Mateo." Alexis's small dog ran up and situated itself so that its butt ended up near Joseph's face. The dog first fell asleep, then Alexis, then Joseph, next to a woman in a thong and no top. Sleep came in uncomfortable, fitful waves.

Another night, Joseph had just gotten in bed at Substance, and his phone rang. Alexis was crying. "I don't know where they are," she wailed. "I can't find my keys." Joseph could hear her rattle her door. "I can't find my fucking keys. I can't get in. I'm locked out. Oh fuck, Joseph, help me. Help me."

"Okay, Alexis, don't go anywhere...I'll be over." It took only a minute to get there—Alexis lived close, in an apartment complex on Leary Way—and when Joseph arrived he could see her through the window, slumped against her apartment door. Her things littered the hallway, her head tilted down against her chest. Alexis got up and wobbled toward him, mascara going in streaks down her face. Her hair looked as if it had been styled at the beginning of the night, but by then was at war with itself, brushed and coifed in spots, wild and fluffed in others. She half-ran to the door, pounding her feet on the ground, and hung on Joseph like a heavy yoke. With her silk blouse against him, wearing tight jeans and gold jewelry he'd never seen her wear, she started sobbing.

"Joseph, I don't know where they are. Fuck. Please help."

Not knowing what else to do, Joseph took her back to Substance, and the short car ride calmed her. He strapped her arm around his shoulder, dragged her inside. In his room she stripped, fully bare for the first time.

"Hold me, Joseph. Just hold me." Alexis reached out like a child from under the covers. Joseph hugged her, but almost as soon as he did, Alexis began to snore. Maybe in the morning, he thought, they would wake. Warm and refreshed, they could finally be one.

In the morning, Alexis still slept. Joseph had to leave. Walking out of the house, he agonized over their chance passing, then in the next second agonized over entertaining that chance and not being with Bethany. All these agonies kept overlapping.

By the afternoon, Joseph had received two voice mails from Alexis, one profusely thanking him for taking her in, the other admitting she had done her best, but she just wasn't sure if all the vomit on his bedroom floor was gone.

14

Joseph and Bethany saw each other more regularly after the debacle of keys and vomit. Joseph began to tell Bethany intimate things, like when his sister had a baby and named it Anne, though most often he talked about his new boss at the package delivery company, Mike. Details of Wyoming, the pickup, those things he left out, as if telling her anything from the past would spoil their future. Often in that time Bethany biked over to Substance and entered Joseph's room, and he always loved the underwear she wore, sometimes printed with animals, sometimes just red and white stripes, but always a blend of innocent and exciting. Everything they did, Joseph imagined, was easier than it would have been with anyone else, even with Mary. Though he never asked Bethany how she knew so much, or how she did it all so effortlessly. She was a passionate person, pretty enough to experiment with whomever she wanted to experiment with back home. Joseph entertained the possibility that all of her interest in base ventures had been stored up, and she was releasing it all on someone who bore the mark of a lucky guy more than anyone else on the planet. Tony Chester himself could not compare.

Yet still there was Alexis. Joseph still, every so often, went over to her place and rubbed her back and they wrestled. Perhaps, it could be reasoned, he did this because he wanted to prove to the guys in South Dakota that he could get a hot girl from California, someone they could never dream of being with while living in their small farming town with their acne-faced, big-boned farmer's daughter of a wife. Though even that fails to make sense, since Jarvis and Austin and Brady and all the rest would never come close to meeting Alexis, and Joseph knew that.

Also there was what happened parallel to both Bethany and Alexis. Everyone at the house of women had, by then, paired up. Laurel and Tina and Crystal and a home-schooled Christian girl from Walla Walla, Amelia Birds, another who lived there. Through a dating website Laurel found Boris Trevor, who worked at Boeing and wore bike tights into bars and parted his hair down the middle. Amelia was with a math professor, whom she met via a God-centric dating website. And Crystal was with Darrin, a lawyer, while Tina began her lifelong relationship with Bob, as everyone assumed it would be.

Jennifer Loren was the fifth member of their house, and the first memory Joseph has of her is in the living room the night of the broken guitar. That evening, Jennifer was like a ghost, sneaking in to retrieve a pair of knitting needles and leaving right after, going down the hall without a word.

Jennifer always did her own thing, painting in the basement or gardening in the backyard. She never laughed at Joseph's jokes, and he assumed she didn't care. That's how it was, until one day, at the beginning of summer, it dawned on him that Jennifer was pretty and unattached. Even if she worked with Tina and Bethany building houses for the poor, he could see her. He could see every person alive. Jennifer conveyed a meek and gentle spirit, and she would not tell a soul. More and more, Joseph lost his grip on reality.

"I love Jennifer," Bethany told Joseph. They lay in her rickety bed, a longboard propped up in the corner. Joseph was kissing Bethany's long stomach. She played with his hair. He still had hair then. "Whatever guy ends up with her is going to be so lucky. I'd understand if you want to be with her instead of me."

Joseph just kissed her more, lower, and with more intent, and Bethany did not say another word. Not until after, listening to her sleep, did he begin to wonder why Bethany said such things. In an ideal world it made no sense to her that men did not line up for Jennifer, who was, as Bethany said, "perfect in every way." When in reality Bethany knew Jennifer was not as beautiful as she—as almost all women were not—but, by saying Jennifer was, Bethany absolved herself of guilt for participating in a world she feigned to protest. Whatever the case, that little sentence in bed was enough to send Joseph down a dangerous path.

It happened like a dream, it seemed to Joseph, how they arranged to watch a comedy show on DVD, and as he pulled up on the street above the house of women, he still did not have a plan. On a Friday night, the sun going down, Mount Rainier stood out clearly. Joseph got out of the car, legs went forward, but not because he told them to. Even as he approached, he told himself nothing would happen. Nothing that would lead into something they'd later have to explain to others. But as Jennifer opened the door, everything dissolved. She wore a stretchy skirt and a blouse around her large breasts, swollen as if readying themselves for nursing. The rest of her body was slim, and "mistakes" is all he saw in front of him. The shades drawn, he had the thought, as they sat down, that Jennifer, who looked at him with a hopeful smile, had engineered the hypnotic ambience of the room.

The movie started, and Joseph kept telling himself there would be no reward for letting what was about to happen happen. But he had yet to go through what he needed to go through, or God had determined long ago that this would happen, because at that moment Joseph Bethel inched closer. Any more and he would breach an unspoken hull, one only to be mended with conversations about how they'd be "better off as friends." Then he did it, and as they held hands Jennifer was content, resting her head on Joseph's shoulder like there was nobody else in the world. A time machine, he thought, I need a time machine.

Joseph's birthday came soon after and his mom and dad came to Seattle to celebrate.

"The flight was good," Mom said on the phone. "We can't wait to see you."

Joseph was walking through the airport to meet them at the baggage carousel, feeling the same, in a way, but in another he wished his parents would take the next flight back to South Dakota and never think of him again. By the revolving steel he surprised Mom by taking her by the shoulders, making her whip around. And when she saw her son for the first time in almost half a year, tears filled her eyes. No longer could she make him breakfast omelets or wash his jeans, but she hugged him tightly, because she could still do that. Someone nearby gave them a queer look. Turns out, it was someone Dad had talked to on the flight.

"Didn't get any height from mom and dad, did he?"

"Oh yeah, he's tall, isn't he," Mom said.

"Almost as tall as his dad," Dad said, several inches shorter. He gave Joseph a certain hug, putting one arm around his son and patting him on the back a couple times. "Good to see you there, bud."

Joseph did his best to smile but was thinking of the dent and of Bethany, how if he had resolved it right away and not fooled around with any others, everything would have been so much better at that moment. Leaving the concourse, the two South Dakotan parents were impressed that their son could drive down the winding circle of the parking garage and out into the damp overcast without directions. They barely spoke, too agog to see Joseph navigating his way around a city they never had taken him. So much so that Mom would later repeat, to anyone who asked about the trip, "He just zipped around the city, like it was no big deal."

On the way back they stopped at Dick's—Bill Gates's favorite burger place—and though Mom and Dad were not used to long lines for fast food, they waited anyway, eating the greasy meat and thick milkshakes in the car.

"Pretty good burger," Dad said, and that made Joseph happy, to start them off with something they liked.

At Substance, being so tired from the trip, they went to bed right away, with Mom offering to sleep on the floor. Even if it meant her back being wrecked for months, she would have done it, but Joseph didn't allow her to and set up the air mattress for himself. After they fell asleep, he snuck out to the backyard. There was a sidewalk connecting to a mother-in-law guest house where Substance's landlord lived, and while listening to Bethany's voice, Joseph ached, regretting almost every decision he ever made. The next morning there was work at the package delivery company, but he took the day off from waxing boats. Back at Substance, after throwing brown boxes into trucks, Mom was in the bathroom finishing her makeup. Dad stood in Joseph's room, pushing the mattress down.

"The bed's working out for you then? Did that guy help you unload it all?"

They had talked about Joseph's furniture and what it cost and whether he got a good deal or not. "It didn't take long," Joseph said. "Worked well, I thought."

"Well, it's here now."

Joseph did not want to argue. "All right," he said, changing the subject. "I need to shower, then we can go on our tour? What do you guys think?"

"Sounds like a plan, my boy," Mom said from the bathroom. Joseph moved his head from his doorway to see her put down her curling iron. She gave her dirty son a hug.

"Gotta shower, Mom." Joseph patted her on the back, so she let go, but it looked as if she could have held on for much longer, maybe infinitely.

To Elliott Bay Marina first, where Joseph waxed boats. The air burst with wood chips and grass as they strolled on the promenade near the boathouse. They could see out into the sound where a cruise ship dominated the water, out beyond the hundreds of docked boats. Beyond that, downtown, and the sunlight glimmering off the glass structures. Joseph pointed to Queen Anne Hill to the east.

"That's so pretty," Mom said, and for a second Joseph thought he knew what it was like for someone with a good job to show his parents what he does for a living.

"There's a park over there. It's where they take all the postcard pictures of Seattle. You guys wanna go?"

"Your deal," Dad said. "We can go wherever."

"Let's do it." So Joseph gathered up Mom and Dad and they followed him like two baby chicks to the car.

At the bottom of the hill Joseph was glad to find a place where he did not have to parallel park. The screaming thoughts looped in his head. He wished to be free from them, with Bethany at his side.

"Yes, Mother, it is quite nice," Joseph imagined, wrapping his arm around Bethany with curly hair. She looked up with utter affection as Dad patted a good, prosperous son on the back.

In the realness of day they trudged up the hill, and Joseph sensed the weight of Mom and Dad's journey. Sweat came from their brows. More and more, they fell behind.

"I don't know, guys," Joseph said, slowing down so they could catch up. "I don't know where I'm going, exactly. I've only been here once, and you guys don't need to walk all over the place."

"The view over at the boats was fine for me. And this is beautiful right here." With her hands on her hips, Mom could not have seen more than a city block.

"Yeah, bud," Dad said, his voice strained from the exertion. "We're here to do whatever."

"Let's go back then, we've got more walking to do on our library trip." Joseph was trying to make it light, for himself and for them.

"Yeah," Dad said as they went back down, "you're walking us across the country out here."

Dad gave a wry smile, which meant he was pleased, while Mom put her arm around her son's waist. "We'll find it next time we come out," she said, and for reasons he did not understand, that almost made Joseph cry.

One of his favorite places in the city helped, the pho restaurant in Ballard. With his parents on the other side of the booth, Joseph demonstrated how to eat the soup with chopsticks. He got the large, ordering Mom the small and Dad the medium, making them three little bears. They gave the foreign utensils a try, for a minute or two, until giving up and resorting to a spoon and a fork. After soup they took a long walk to the library in Fremont, where just up the hill is the Troll. Before Joseph left for Seattle, Mom had said, "Take lots of pictures," and that rang in his ears, as he never did. He could not bring himself to take pictures of his life until everything was right. But as they walked Joseph felt better, because he believed Mom felt better. This trip provided for her the photographs he never took. Overgrown plants and flowers sprouted from the moist soil and the click, click, clicking of Mom's manual camera sounded in their ears. On the way back from the library Mom took a picture of Joseph walking next to Dad. In the picture Joseph is tall and fit, and carries with him a cloth satchel of CDs from the library. That photo is around, somewhere, Joseph knows, in his parents' old house. He has seen it once or twice over the years, but he can't bear seeing it again, as it always reminds him of lost time.

They went to bed early that evening, and from his foam padding on the floor, Joseph laughed along with Mom after Dad made a joke about how sore he was from walking all day. In the next moment, Joseph heard, "Stop laughing, you selfish fuck. There are pickups with dents you have not fixed. Are you that dumb?" Joseph became quiet as a stone.

Everett in the morning, to see a cousin Mom visited as a child. Mom sat in the back of Joseph's car and acted as the navigator as the men in front talked sports, and that drive might be one of the last drives Joseph ever took where he did not fear for his life and the lives of every other person on the road. Mom and Dad stabilized their boy, that one last time. In Everett with Mom's cousin, they toured the islands off the coast and ate delicious seafood, though Dad seemed most impressed with the lack of mosquitoes. The last night, the adults sitting by the indoor fireplace, Joseph into the nearby woods. On a Saturday night, he spoke with Bethany, who partied outside Redmond at an end-of-the-year event for all the house builders.

"Here, let me get out of this kitchen," she said, then a pause. Joseph picked at the bark of a tree. "So you're in Everett?" she asked in a quieter place than before. "Are you having a good time with your parents?"

"For sure, it's good seeing them. And it's pretty up here, but I don't understand why anyone would want to live here. I mean, Seattle is so close."

"I like having you in Seattle, Joseph Bethel. You should've been here tonight."

"Why's that?"

"Oh, actually, it's so bad, I shouldn't tell you."

"What is it?" Joseph threw a stick, his mind absent of anything else, a state he took for granted less and less as the years went by.

"Oh my gosh, okay. So we had this thing after supper where they went around and picked out different parts of the essays we wrote to apply for AmeriCorps."

"Uh, okay, that sounds a little wrong."

"It wasn't so bad, but I can't tell you what I wrote, Joseph. It's so embarrassing."

Joseph knew little of drinking, but he did know that if a person's demeanor improves when partaking, it is a good sign of their character. Bethany had been drinking and she was genial as always. "What was it?" he asked.

"No, I can't. It's too much."

"I bet it's not that bad, Beth. You can tell me."

Bethany started, then stopped. "I'll tell you when you get back...okay?"

"Sounds good."

"Oh Joseph, I'm so tired right now. I wish you were here. I..." Then there was a second where Bethany put the phone down. "Whoops, sorry. Somebody's yelling for me, Joe. I should mosey. But you're top-notch, all right? Bye-bye."

"Goodnight, Bethany." Joseph clicked the end button on his phone and walked to the house, following a light in the distance. He fell asleep with Bethany on his mind.

In the morning the Bethels left for a hotel in Tukwila, and as they drove Joseph thought about Bethany, what he'd wanted to tell her the night before: of marriage, someday, when everything was all worked out. He wanted to tell Mom and Dad the whole story too, from birth to the dent, and after it was done he saw in his mind Mom taking his hand, considering it a blessing to hear her son's heartfelt thoughts, then, before getting to the hotel, convincing him everything would be okay. Dad would've called ten insurance agents by then, even the man with the pickup. But Joseph couldn't do it. He just put on his happiest face.

At the hotel, Mom and Dad encouraged Joseph to call his new friends. So he got a hold of Laurel and Jennifer, but not Bethany. If someone had pressed Joseph then, he might've said Bethany was a secret, or she was in another way too young, but what's most likely is she seemed too good, and since Mary the thought of being with someone like Bethany in a lasting way was for those who believed in miracles, which Joseph no longer did. So Laurel and Jennifer came, giving birthday hugs and smelling of suntan lotion. Two, he thought, is that not always better than one? They went out through the lobby and into the sunny outdoors.

At poolside the young women unwrapped their towels and displayed their slender bodies. They dipped their toes in the water as Joseph swam around. In between gulps of air he caught glimpses of Jennifer's pneumatic frame, not totally covered by a two-piece. Normally she shrouded her figure in work boots, caulk-covered blue jeans, heavy t-shirts and coats. But that afternoon she gave Joseph a glorious display. And Laurel too, her pale skin and auburn hair, her freckled breasts, made Joseph think he'd made the right choice. He swam, letting the water and sun numb his brain.

In the coolness of the air conditioning they ate pizza as they watched the Twins play against the Mariners. The chlorine mixed with the smell of cheese and sauce, and Joseph could not help but be reminded of other birthdays he'd loved, how this was even better with two beautiful women his age. Dad asked questions about their lives and jobs, though mostly they seemed to want to compliment Joseph.

"Your son is really funny," Laurel said. Jennifer nodded her head with a mouthful of pizza. "We love having him in Seattle."

For a bit, Joseph was embarrassed, but then he looked up and Mom was looking right back at him with a surprised kind of happiness, as if her son had become a man. The one he should have become, what was it, years ago?

15

Then came a promotion at the package delivery company, a day after Joseph's birthday. About a month before, a bald man, with wisps of stray hairs combed over his pillow of a head, had administered Joseph's interview for a position called Operational Management Specialist. Impressive-sounding in name, it meant Joseph would become the intermediary between the oligarchy of upper management and the proletariat of drivers—though the drivers, because of the union, made as much money as many of those in management. In the end, the OMS would make sure the trucks came in each day and all the packages got delivered and the time cards got sent in through the computer. Take the shit, in other words. It was not a full-time position but it came with the promise of developing into one. If Joseph stuck with it, he could make package distribution a career. In his near future, he saw the possibility of a job paying well enough to make worries about dents seem irrelevant.

With the good news, Joseph was ready to celebrate the Fourth of July, gladly accepting Bethany's invitation to enjoy the holiday at her place. First, there would be another party on the same day with William, who waxed boats with Joseph. William lived near Lake Union in the Eastlake neighborhood, so the three of them, Joseph and William and William's girlfriend, went down to a dock, jutting out and over the water. They watched as hundreds of boats readied themselves for the fireworks, tying together in a metastasizing knot. The warm afternoon turned into a cool evening, and William's girlfriend, an Asian-American twentysomething from Madison, cuddled up to her man. More than once, she slapped William on the butt playfully; they seemed to Joseph the picture of life. At a picnic table, with guacamole and chips and beers, a last orange light shimmered on the water as longer shadows followed those passing by, sunglasses resting on their heads. That's when William and his girlfriend began to canoodle, which Joseph took as his cue to leave. They said goodbye, and the single man walked up the hill to Eastlake Avenue, where traffic was bumper-to-bumper. On foot, his pace quicker than the cars. Passing over the University Bridge, to Bethany's corner and her tan house squished between others, close to dark, and up her carpeted steps, Joseph heard the house builders over beat-heavy music, smelled grilled meat. A slight breeze came through the place as someone yelled, "Fer 'Merica."

When it came time for fireworks they climbed on the roof by way of a wobbly ladder. Sitting on the eroding shingles, they were given a glorious view of the city. Explosions in the sky lit their faces as Joseph and Bethany toyed with each other's fingers behind their backs. Headley was there that night, someone Joseph liked a great deal, the way he animatedly ranted about the woes of the Mariners and Seattle's transit system.

"Please," Joseph thought to himself, "ask Jennifer out." He wanted someone to cover his mistakes. Jennifer was on the roof as well, a few down the row. But Headley just took a drink of beer and gesticulated as he commented on the fireworks to some of the others, and Jennifer stayed quiet. They had not had a closet make-out, drunk and falling on top of each other. They'd held hands while watching a movie. The only way out now was through heartache. Even without God, Joseph did not entertain shades of gray.

After the fireworks, and after the rest of the partiers left, Bethany and Joseph went to her room. When they finished finishing each other they had their goodbye on the landing. Above them hung a framed secondhand painting of an Indian with a headdress. Someone in the house had named him Bruce.

"You're something, Joseph Bethel." Bethany's neck was littered with small red spots. A step above Joseph, she gave him a kiss on the top of his head where he still had hair, even if more and more Joseph knew God plucked it away as the debt to the owner of a pickup went unpaid.

"Good luck getting to your car," she said, wearing nothing but small underwear. He walked down the stairs and waved up at her. "Goodnight," she mouthed.

Joseph's car was about two miles away, though every step was necessary. Each one sweeping away dust in his mind, brushing down to the spotless floor of the decision. That night at Substance, Joseph emailed Jennifer. They should talk, he wrote, and she agreed. Just two days later, in the evening under a big tree near the house of women, at the end of some rambling mumbles, Joseph said the most important thing. To let Jennifer know they'd be going no further, that what they'd already done was a mistake.

"But I want us to keep being friends," he said. Jennifer nodded politely and walked him to his car where they hugged goodbye. Joseph drove north knowing the hard work was done.

That same evening, Joseph and Bethany meandered on a bike path along Lake Union. Nighttime, and that day Bethany had straightened her hair. It transformed her into a model, Joseph thought, rather than the usual look of uncaring but naturally beautiful hippie, or, on some days, a teenager in an advertisement for volumizing shampoo.

"What made you decide to do that?" Joseph asked, his heart pounding.

"I don't know." Bethany ran her fingers through the straightness. "I just get sick of curls sometimes. Makes me look like a baby."

"I don't think so. I mean, you look good now with your hair like this. Don't worry about changing it for me."

"I didn't," Bethany said. "I don't. Anyway, like I said, I just don't like it sometimes."

They neared Gas Works Park, and that's when Joseph started to explain what had happened. After finishing with his second set of rambling mumbles of the day, he came to the thing he most wanted to tell Bethany.

"Now it'll be me and you. That's what I want."

Bethany tensed. Her posture changed her tone, away from effervescence to a more strained agitation.

"You're making this dramatic, Joseph. I told you before we started I didn't want to be in some drama. That's what this is."

And it could have been the infidelity, however small—as Bethany must have thought before that no one would ever cheat on her—but she ran. Her run was unmistakable, Joseph had it memorized from when they played catch. She wore sandals and a sarong, so she didn't go fast, and for a moment he thought of taking off to catch her. Then she hiked up her long skirt and her sandals flew off and her run became a full sprint. So Joseph jogged, every foot on the ground a reminder of his stupidity. Maybe if he had come to the city with more experience, things would be different.

"Lord God," he said out loud. "I should be in her bedroom with beers right now. She should be laughing her laugh. We should be naked."

A crystal clear night. Joseph peered ahead, straining to see the outline of Bethany's lanky frame. He came upon the hill overlooking the lake. From the top he could see no one. He went to the concrete barrier against the water, like a pew cut into the land. The view was tiny red dots from cars intersecting the downtown skyline and skyscrapers reflecting off the lake. To the west, Capitol Hill with its trees on top of houses on top of apartments on top of more houses. Bobbing houseboats, buoyed in every direction, and the sound of steady pushing of waves. The humming of the interstate. For another hour Joseph searched but never found her. He considered even going to Bethany's place, but his presence would not be welcomed, that much he knew. With nowhere else to go, he went to his car—parked on the street—and listened to sports radio on the softest volume. At some point in the morning he started his car and lurched away, feeling, for the first time, keenly responsible for someone else's safety. For once in his life Joseph knew what it was like to be a man. Like everything else, when it finally came for Joseph Bethel, it came when he did not want it to.

16

As a way of finding solace, Joseph started seeing more of Micah Doppler, the husband of Polly Bell. They'd met years before at a Christian music magazine in Texas where Joseph interned. Doppler was the managing editor of the magazine, and often that summer—and later in Seattle—used words like cunctation in ordinary sentences. It came naturally, Joseph reasoned. The man was smarter than most. The only problem, again in Texas and when they reunited in Seattle, is that Micah also qualified the things he said by reiterating he was "not trying to be mean." Then, after saying the thing that just tore down the other person, Micah would stand there, a tall man with flabby but skinny arms and a full head of stringy brown hair, and oddly stare at the less intelligent person—Joseph more than once—as if it were a chore to hear words other than his own.

Polly Bell grew up in Austin and met Micah through church, making their beginnings auspicious. Micah was a

PK—preacher's kid—who worked out his salvation at the forefront of the emerging church movement in the late '90s, starting a music and religion website while stationed in South Dakota at Ellsworth Air Force Base. He called it "Godoppler," and it did not surprise Joseph when he found out that Micah would mix his own name with God's. Micah parlayed the website into the job at the magazine in Texas, and it was there he met Polly, and they then started a relationship guided by, in part, a shared belief in Jesus Christ.

Polly was sweet to Joseph, the few times they talked that Texas summer. Busty, with blue eyes and chipmunk cheeks, she must have been born with a rebellious streak, if willing to see someone like Micah. While he was a professed Christian, someone who could be taken home to her parents, Micah also smoked weed almost every day and talked of polyamorous relationships being superior to monogamous ones. Shortly after that summer Micah quit the magazine, because of what he told Joseph were "irreconcilable differences." In reality, it was more dramatic than that, with Micah leaving Texas after mass emailing everyone in his address book a lengthy diatribe, detailing the ways in which the publisher was a massive failure and the publisher's wife was the Antichrist.

Micah could be vindictive and mean, and Joseph knew that, but also he could not stop being thankful to his onetime editor, long after the two stopped talking on a regular basis. Micah knew, very personally, the same struggles. It was after Suzanne that Joseph called out to Seattle, where Micah and Polly lived as a married couple, and though they had not talked in years, Micah said the words that made sense, validating

Joseph's exasperation instead of parroting the rote lines from those in the church, pointing out how it was "incredibly convenient for married people to say that they were the only ones who patiently waited on God's timing."

With so much in common with the man, Joseph could never stop hoping they'd one day be best friends. So Joseph was happy, after the park, that he and Micah got to spend more time together. One evening they went to play poker at Headley's basement apartment in Capitol Hill. By the bus stop outside an Afghani restaurant, an American flag waved. A perfectly calm evening, yet Joseph stood there nervous. At any second a question would arise, and Micah would tilt his head, and Joseph would know he'd been outed as a fraud. As they waited for the bus they discussed college majors, since Micah planned on going back to school, and always Micah was going back to school, always choosing a different profession, each one more abstract than the last.

"So you know about personality disorders then?" Micah asked. Joseph could not determine whether he had been asked a question or issued a challenge to list as many as he could. He decided to answer with a question.

"Yeah, which ones?" The sun set as cars drove by on 45th Street.

"Mind you," Micah said, "I am not an expert. But I was wondering about classifying someone I am mostly sure is a borderline personality. What kind of behaviors would you use to quantify that?"

"Yeah, that's interesting." Joseph was stalling. "I'd say like an inability to separate his fantasy life from, you know, real life?"

"Right. I didn't mean to put you on the spot here, Joseph…" Then they had a moment of silence. Joseph remembered very little from his studies in college and knew at that moment he was nowhere near being right. He wanted to make a joke but he couldn't, not unless Polly was there. She provided levity, shaping Micah into a better version of himself.

"That's neat they fly that," Joseph said, desperate to change the subject. "After all the stuff they went through after 9/11? I'm sure people were jerks at first, but they still love America."

Micah responded by giving Joseph a look a professor might give a student who is unable to answer a rudimentary question. "If you don't know why they have that flag up, Joseph, I can't explain it."

Thankfully, right then the bus came, and they did not speak on the ride. That night with Micah was uncomfortable for Joseph, like many others, yet they got over it and had a fine enough time, like they always did, with Joseph just happy to be around Micah, cherishing any new wisdom that might fall out of his elder's mouth. What was harder to get over, at least for Micah, was the problem of loving only one woman, something Joseph understood, in a way, but in another never even came close.

Without thinking of the consequences, Joseph invited Alexis and Micah to go out. Micah's friend, who played in a well-known band in Seattle, showed up as well, at a medieval-themed soccer bar in Fremont that played European soccer league games on Saturday and Sunday mornings. Sitting at a table by an unlit fireplace, they could have been assessed by others at the bar as pretentious: Micah's lectures, the band boy checking his phone, Alexis with her overly stylized glasses, and

Joseph, trying his best to appear important. William's arrival, along with his girlfriend, tempered the group.

"There are so many ways," Micah was explaining to William, though the whole group listened. "Polyamory is just another one. Our culture is so far behind Europe. And I don't want to say it's the correct way, necessarily, but it's a way of experiencing love more people should consider. Of course, you know the media shoves it down our throat, all the husband and wife patriarchal nonsense. I'm not talking about the backward shit they do in Utah either. I want us to have a discourse on adult love between consenting people. Listen, do you know about the bonobos?"

"Nah," William said, taking a drink of beer. "Or wait, are those the apes that love to fuck?"

Micah laughed. Joseph rarely saw Micah laugh. "That's close, actually. Bonobos are the apes who live in Central Africa. They're rare, but scientists have found them to be a peaceful ape, unlike other subspecies that kill their young. Not the bonobos. They resolve their conflict by fucking. I believe we can all be like that, as long as we strip ourselves of all the neo-con bullshit that infects our culture."

William was rapt. Micah went on to explain that he and his wife were not only experimenting with polyamory but had become immersed in the practice. "That's why I wear the wedding band on my right hand." Micah laid his hand on the gouged table. "As a sign of our love, but also my openness to all love."

Everyone drank, Alexis the most, and at some point she got Micah and Joseph to arm-wrestle. As they gripped hands over the slippery beer-ringed table, Micah whispered to Joseph, "Let me win," and Joseph considered that for a millisecond before besting his mentor. Alexis cheered for more.

"No thanks." Joseph stretched his arm to allay the disappointed look he received. "We're not your sideshow, babe."

"Aww, too bad," she said, and started texting. Micah went back to William, and Joseph to Emma, William's girlfriend. They talked about her job downtown over the loud music. Soon, the band boy left, then William and Emma. But the night went on. Micah and Alexis were competing to see who could drink more, diving deeper and deeper into Alexis's amorphous sexuality. Micah assured her of the beauty of a polyamorous relationship. When she left for the bathroom, Micah leaned in to Joseph. He didn't speak until very close.

"So," he said, "I don't know if you've been in a threesome before, but they're not bad, especially with someone you know."

"Ha, what?" Joseph said.

"Trust me, you can do it."

"Uh, I don't know, man. I don't think that's my style."

Though as Micah took a drink of his beer, giving a side-eyed glance, Joseph began to wonder if saying no meant missing out once more, like with Claire in Brookings. Were all these sexual adventures happening without him? And would they only ever be available long before he understood what to do? Alexis came back from the bathroom.

"So," Micah said, "you guys wanna go watch a movie or something? It's getting loud in here." Alexis shook her head yes and left for a smoke, letting Joseph and Micah pay the bill.

Only a few minutes in her studio apartment and one of the participants found himself stepping backward toward the door, careful not to stomp on Mateo, the small dog. With Alexis's naked back to him, Joseph took account of her butterfly tattoo. At that moment it seemed more dangerous, almost like a bat. Then, as Micah tossed Alexis on the bed, the same one she and Joseph watched movies on, the door opened and he hurried down the hallway, doing his best to not hear any noises. He knew they would haunt him, if he did. Bethany, Joseph jogged down the hall and out of the building, Bethany was the only shot at happiness in this life. The very next day her voice mail greeting met Joseph with a predictable sunniness.

"Hi Bethany," Joseph said to the machine. "I don't know what you're doing tonight, but I'd like to see you. I wasn't trying to be dramatic, really, I wanted to be honest. Please call me. I have some news." Even though he had no news and did not expect a call, later that night, his head lay on Bethany's stomach, and he listened to her ocean. She stroked his hair. A map of the world was taped on the wall above Bethany's twin bed, and as he fell asleep Joseph dreamed of where they would one day go.

It was good being back together. Bethany helped neutralize the pain of being the operational management specialist. Joseph would never tell his dad how much he hated the job; instead in their conversations it was just "tough getting used to" or "working in management is definitely different than working as an hourly worker." What Joseph wanted to say is he hated being the OMS as much as he'd hated anything before, and a lot of that had to do with the one in charge. Mike

Terry was, to Joseph, a cartoon villain, someone thought up by a pasty animator who, in high school, was viciously bullied and later looked to exorcise demons. At first, though, it wasn't that bad. In the beginning weeks on the job, Mike Terry treated Joseph flippantly, like hopeless, and therefore not worth knowing, new meat entering boot camp. Joseph was also very busy doing his best to soak in everything he could: names of the drivers, protocol, abbreviations like PCIS, GTS, IGATE, ODS, ODSE, DIAD, DCS, ETT, SOCS, DFUS, DNED, each one with real meaning. Around that time, at five in the evening, a few hours into the OMS shift, Mike sat in a steel chair in the cement office and looked at Joseph like a stern college basketball coach might look at a practice squad freshman. Robert Bones, another middle manager, sat beside Mike as a lapdog sits next to its master.

"So where did you come from again?" Mike blatantly adjusted his testicles inside a pair of tan slacks, slinky ones bought at a golf clothing store.

"South Dakota," Joseph answered, sounding unsure that really was where he came from.

Mike rolled his eyes. "Fuck. That's great. South Dakota." And Mike tapped Robert, and Robert knew then he was supposed to laugh, so he did. "Where did you come from? In the building, preload, twilight?" Mike talked slowly and used sign language, though it was clear he did not know sign language.

"Oh, right," Joseph said. "Preload. I…"

"Fucking preload," Mike said. "Did you get the right packages in the right cars?"

"I think so," Joseph replied.

"Hopefully you'll do better here," Mike said, as if he had not heard a word.

After that it got much worse. The responsibility mounted and Joseph could expect each day a tirade on "fucking the dog" on this or "fucking the dog" on that. It made the still intrepid young employee retreat to another world wherein Joseph imagined Mike's wife wearing layers of makeup to appear young, and how jealous Mike would be, probably get an erection on the spot, if Bethany came into the office. It was the one thing giving Joseph enough strength to stay at the package delivery company.

"It's pretty tough going," Joseph told Bethany after work another night. She had come over to Substance. They saw each other regularly. "There's like sixty drivers I have to learn. I'll get through it, though. We'll get through it."

Bethany, her sarong and top and sandals on the floor, in nothing but the faultless body God gave her, did not need to speak a word to comfort him. Her body and presence did that without utterance. Being with her brought Joseph to a peace with the decisions he'd made so far in life. If they brought him to her, they had been the right ones after all.

17

For reasons not known even to himself, Joseph started perusing Jennifer again. When cornered with the thought he told himself he did it to drown out God's, or Satan's, or whoever's voice it was speaking to him about the dent, which he had not resolved and each day grew more anxious thinking about. With the elegant simplicity of someone like Bethany, there was too much time to hypothesize how it'd all soon go wrong. He could make it go wrong himself.

A rock show approached, and since only those over twenty-one could get in, it'd be impossible to bring Bethany. It only made sense, Joseph aggressively persuaded himself, to call Jennifer. So they met outside the club downtown and waited on the sidewalk, sitting in chairs like Parisians on the Champs-Élysées, watching the line for the sold-out show queue up longer and longer. Joseph had prepared for that, believing anything that interested him would always sell out. Sometimes it did, and sometimes it did not. Jennifer was quiet, and seemed devoted to Joseph for reasons he did not understand. She wore a flannel, one that could be worn to bed—white with red and green flowers—with jeans painted to her body, and a pair of sliding moccasins.

When the doors opened, they went in together. After a few drinks, as the band played instrumental, percussive music, with the drummer's cymbal up in the air and crashing with dramatic regularity, the lead singer sampling his voice through a computer and looping over the beats, Joseph forgot about his choices. Looking over at Jennifer, he saw she was pretty. Everything was fine. The show was great. When it was over they emerged into the black-and-white downtown, and before going their separate ways, they found a quiet street corner and kissed goodbye. As Joseph rode home, with no other passengers on the bus, he hit his head against the window over and over, hard enough so it would hurt.

The very next day, Bethany learned the University of Washington had denied her admission and she would have to settle for Western Washington University. If that plan had failed, her next choice was to stay for another year in Seattle building houses. Joseph liked that idea. Bethany would stay, and after that, who knew? Maybe Mike would leave the package delivery company and a better position than operational management specialist would open up, something good enough so he could provide for Bethany. Maybe help with her tuition. Bellingham was over a hundred miles to the north of Seattle, and Joseph dreaded the thought of Bethany living with guys who called each other bro and got high in the afternoon and snowboarded at night.

Before leaving for school, near the end of summer, she took an expedition to a remote island off the coast of Vancouver to learn about the wildlife. From there, she wrote Joseph an email:

> Sorry I haven't called. I don't have access to a phone at all here and this is my 2nd time on the internet. How are you by the way? Anyway, I'm having a really good time. I've seen orcas, humpback whales, eagles like crazy, sea lions, and I just saw a bear a few minutes ago. Amazing. The people are fantastic...Well, there are a bunch of them who want to use this computer, so I better go. I don't think I'm going to get another chance to check my email, but I'll call you when I get back. Ciao for now.

Sure enough, back from the island that Saturday morning, Bethany did call, and Joseph did go over to see her. Up her stairs, under the framed painting of the Indian named Bruce, on a summer afternoon where everything in the world burst with green and blue. The windows open and no one else home, Joseph heard sloshing in the bathroom. He knocked on the door.

"Hello," he said softly. He sensed Bethany on the other side, her hair resting on the water and the sun lighting the room. Water moved in the tub.

"Oh boy, heeey, so there weren't any showers up there, Joe. I kind of stink. Doing you a favor, buddy. Be out in a little bit."

"Are you hungry? I could go and get us something to eat?"

"Oh my gosh, Joseph, that'd be awesome. But you don't have to."

"You have to be hungry. How about taco truck?"

"That sounds so good, Joseph. But really you don't have to..."

"I'll be right back." And he left. He knew what she liked.

Joseph on an idyllic day, walking the couple blocks to the taco truck, knowing he could provide sustenance for Bethany. It might be a good thing to help her transition into the independent period of life. Returning with the burritos like a proud father, he half-jogged, then went back up her stairs, skipping several steps. In the openness of the living room, he called her name.

"In the bedroom," Bethany said. A few weeks before she had moved to the other side of the house, to a room with a view of downtown and the bridge over Lake Union. Joseph put the food on the coffee table and opened the bedroom door to see Bethany wrapped in a white towel. She dropped it with one pinch of her fingers and the sun barreled in as they moved to her small bed, like they'd been waiting their whole lives for it. As they neared the end, Joseph said, "I'm going to come, Bethany, do you want me to stop?"

And as if she had been mulling over that question in Canada, she quickly said "No," and engulfed it all. That may have been the best thing Joseph Bethel could say he ever knew, or saw, or felt.

Later in the living room on that placid afternoon, they ate burritos and drank beers and watched a movie from the green couch. Bethany's head on his lap, Joseph could not think of a more perfect thing. Of course the stillness didn't last, and he was inundated with a million different thoughts with a million different scenarios that would all be his downfall.

18

Plump in a healthy way, Ashley Greaser in fact boasted a ruddy complexion, like a cherished orphan from the movies, her cheeks pinched with a blushed rouge. An internet stranger with a sultry smile, she ate soup across from Joseph as he became more sure her stable boyfriend would pop out from behind a booth, like on one of those reality shows. But there would be no surprises that night. They just ate their soup, having their date. Ashley was new to the city, which accounted for her search for companionship. She worked at a non-profit encouraging citizens to bike more and after the soup they headed to her place. Lying nude next to her, Joseph thought of Bethany, as if that mattered. As if thinking thoughts ever meant anything to anyone.

The summer waned and Joseph kept working on boats in the morning and in the afternoon at the package delivery company. Often, William encouraged Joseph with the idea of finding others from the internet, and usually Joseph laughed it off, as if it had never happened before and never would again, but sometimes he did end up in bedrooms of those he would never see again. On a dreary Sunday morning Bethany left for college. Joseph came over to help and to give her a mix. One he'd given to Mary and one to Suzanne, but this time he made five. Mrs. Fergus, Bethany's mom, was outside arranging her baby's things in the car as Joseph took the CDs out of the pocket of his hooded sweatshirt, along with the accompanying sheets of paper. Each CD needed a track list.

"It's all the songs I've wanted to play for you," Joseph said as Bethany shuffled through them. "I just haven't got a chance yet. You'll be the cool college kid now."

"Bethany, let's go!" they heard, standing under Bruce, and they kissed goodbye.

Weeks later, early in that first semester, Bethany came back to Seattle to visit house-building friends. She called Joseph too, and as he waited at the bay window of the Substance living room he looked like a dog waiting for its master. As Bethany parked her car on the street he imagined what it would be like for her to park her car there all the time, for it to be a fixture of the neighborhood. In his room they watched a movie her roommates in Bellingham had recommended, guys who Bethany said were "really awesome," and, as Joseph feared, did snowboard and smoke weed. To top it off, they ran a screen-printing company. After they finished Bethany got up, taking the burning candle from his desk—the only thing lighting the room—and with her backside jutting out, she turned and curled one finger, a motion Joseph had only ever seen before in movies. He jumped up and followed her to the shower where she washed them both.

A month went by and they did not see each other. Their telephone conversations faded, but Joseph kept calling and asking to see her new place, and eventually Bethany acquiesced. It helped when Joseph said he'd be coming up to see Micah as well, who had started at Western Washington. At thirty-five, Micah no longer fit the appearance of an undergraduate. His GI bill, issued ten years before, verged on expiration. But he had career plans he outlined to Joseph: a minister, a photographer who took nudes of women as portrayed in famous literature scenes, a psychologist who dealt only with troubled ex-Christians. The problem was, according to Micah, the American educational system. It treated students like pieces of commerce.

"Like sausage through a grinder," he'd say. Joseph was glad for Micah's wanderings. They brought him to Bellingham, where Bethany lived.

The day of the visit was gloomy, and the two men, no longer that young, visited a used bookstore, one with high shelves and rows upon rows of hardbound obscure books. It seemed to Joseph the kind of place Micah would love, and he did, as he ended up buying a cryptic tome on the stonemasons.

"This shit is rare," Micah said as they walked out to the deserted sidewalk. "Very fucking hard to find."

Next they went to a Mexican restaurant where Micah detailed the intricacies of the war in Iraq, and, like always, explained why no one is meant to be monogamous. He drank cheap margaritas while Joseph drank a pop and tried to express, backhandedly, without hurting anyone's feelings—as Joseph knew Micah's were fragile—that he did not want to go to the rock show they planned to attend later in the evening. So they could, as Micah had said, "hit on bitches."

"We're happier than ever," Micah told Joseph about Polly. They were divorced, though not separated. "She and I aren't the kind of people who are meant to be married, but it's good to have someone to share things with. That's the point of life, really."

And as they left the restaurant, even though Joseph thought Micah was a liar when it came to the expressions of his heart, he could not get that thought out of his mind. The point of life was to share it with someone. Bethany. Not Mary or Suzanne, it was Bethany. It always had been.

In her ill-lit kitchen, plants everywhere, Bethany on the floor with her back against a lower cupboard, as Micah drank and talked. Joseph bit his fingernails and listened, accepting anything Bethany offered—she had baked a loaf of bread—with a kind of look that he hoped might convey a genuine desire to have a serious talk. Micah ate the bread with butter and drank his Pabst Blue Ribbon. Between drinking and eating, he ranted on. Micah was on his conspiratorial ideas on 9/11 when Bethany found a sliver of dead air. She got up off the floor.

"Guys, I hate to say it, but I really should get to studying."

Micah swilled down the final remnants, and got up as well, while Joseph wished for someone to assassinate Micah. With him there, nothing had been said, or could be. There would be no moment alone, and as they all went to the door, Joseph's body fought him, like a cat about to be dropped in water.

"It was good to meet you, Bethany," Micah said. Both men stood outside. "I can tell you and the people who live here are the smart ones in this dearth of intellects. I'll be back for sure."

Eyes glazed over, Bethany gave Micah a smile, one that could only be recognized as fake. And as she shut the door—Joseph would always remember this—she gave him the same one.

Worms ate at Joseph's stomach as they drove away. There was no way in heaven or on earth he could find the will to go to the rock show. Telling Micah that meant theatrics—some huffing and puffing as Micah got out of the car—but it was the only option. Before leaving Bellingham, Joseph filled up on gas, and when he got back in his car to go he noticed a buzz from his passenger seat. Maybe Micah had put her off. The phone was as close to his ear as it could be.

"I'm sorry for acting weird," Bethany said in her voice mail. "But I was thinking the whole time in the kitchen that we can't keep going. It's not healthy, not for me, and I don't think for you either. I need to start my own life, Joseph. I care for you, and I hope the best for you, whatever you do. But I should go. Take care now. Bye."

Considering everything leading up to that day in Joseph Bethel's life, it is strange how he took the news. He did not immediately call back. He only thought, almost with an eerie calm as he pulled out of the gas station, that there were others.

"I can find someone else," he thought. "I have to give it time."

Bearing such an indifferent attitude, Joseph did not come near understanding, as he hummed south down I-5 to Seattle through a low fog, how he would regret doing nothing that day as much as he would regret anything else for the rest of his forgotten, unremarkable life.

19

They call it peak season. Starting before Thanksgiving, it runs through the New Year. Smack dab in the middle of it, Joseph sat erectly in front of a computer in the dispatch office. Mike was there, in one of two militaristic chairs against the wall, along with a young driver with slicked-back hair who called everyone he liked "bitch."

Black, chalky grime from the trucks' exhaust lacquered the walls, and just outside the door trucks coughed to a stop and parked just feet away, their back ends butting up against a moving belt so the packages could be unloaded and loaded into semis and taken to all different parts of the world. Mike and the young driver "shot the shit," as Joseph faced the computer, finished with time cards for the drivers and their helpers, who came in primarily for that season. It was about seven in the evening. Only a fraction of the hundred or so drivers in; some would not be in for hours still. With nothing else to do,

Joseph turned his chair, crossing his legs. Maybe he could add a word about having a "swinging dick," or share a laugh when the young driver talked about the "fucking gay resort" he had to go to with his girlfriend that Christmas.

"What are you doing?" Mike asked, and Joseph immediately lost his blood. The slicked-back-hair driver chuckled. "Don't you have fucking work to do?"

"I just got done with the last card," Joseph said meekly.

"Last card, huh." Mike looked over at the young driver. "There'd better be no errors tomorrow on those fucking cards, absolutely no fucking errors."

"Shouldn't be," Joseph said, willing himself to stay in the same position, facing the two more assured men. But very soon he turned and let his fake smile relax into a pool of worry.

The next morning the sound of Joseph's phone buzzing on the bedside table. Picking it up in a dream, Joseph hazily recognized the number. This was Harriet Jones, the manager above Mike.

"We're very disappointed," she said in her voice mail. "When you come in, we're going to have to talk about making improvements."

Going to work as the OMS that day, longing for Bethany and hampered with possibly demonic thoughts of unfixed dents, is not where Joseph wanted to be in life, but, he had to admit, it would be better for Harriet to direct the meeting. She was like a grade-school teacher: the worst he'd get from her would be a gentle scolding, playfully slapping Joseph's right hand and telling him to try "a little bit harder" on his handwriting.

"Like I said on the phone," Harriet repeated in her square cement office. Mike paced behind her. "We just can't have these errors when we get here in the morning."

"Yesterday," Mike chimed in. "So yesterday when you were sitting there with your legs up and you told me you had all the time cards perfect, were you lying?" Almost breathless, it appeared as though Mike wanted to lunge over Harriet's desk and strangle Joseph.

"I wasn't, Mike. I honestly thought I had them right. I wouldn't have been talking with you guys if I hadn't."

"But that's the problem," Harriet said, trying to shift the conversation, calm it down. "You have to know they're right, right?" And she even smiled. "Now, Mike and I have talked about this, and we think we have a plan from now until Christmas."

"Every day." Mike picked up the time card with the errors from the previous evening. "On every card I need you to check each box, then I mark it off with this highlighter." Mike streaked the paper with yellow. "That means it's perfect, okay? Then I want a printed copy of that. Staple it with the driver's copy. And if I see you with your legs up and there are time card errors the next day again, we are going to have more than a talk."

Harriet nodded her head, as if condoning violence. "That needs to be done every day, okay, Joseph?" And she gave another smile.

For the rest of that peak season Joseph faced forward and worked. Even if there was nothing to do, he'd click around on random programs until something came along. The only thing keeping him going those late nights was the knowledge that in a couple weeks it would all end. He would go home and see his family. On Christmas Eve, late at night, dark and silent in the warehouse except for the office, Harriet and Mike and Robert talked holiday plans. No one asked Joseph what his were. Lucky, is what he thought, as he would not have to tell them he was going to South Dakota. By then it was clear Mike had done nothing to secure the time off.

"I'll take care of you," Mike had promised in October. It was a distant, forgotten memory.

Snow fell as Joseph arrived in Minneapolis for his connecting flight. And as he disembarked, he thought, since he had no messages, maybe Mike set aside the time after all. Maybe this would be an honest-to-goodness Christmas miracle. Joseph walked through the airport terminal. Almost there, starting to sense a real hope, his phone rang. Seeing the number made Joseph lose a bit of strength in his knees, so he went to sit down in one of the rooms with pay phones no one sits in anymore. He listened to the message in peace.

"Joseph," Robert said. The sound of laughter in the background. "It's about quarter to four. Where you at, buddy, I don't want to have to cover your ass. Call me."

Later, Joseph would wish he'd never called back, that his last day of work at the package distribution company was that day in the airport and he left that OMS job and found for himself, like in a romantic novel, his true calling, maybe even gone to Paris to find it. But that's not how Joseph Bethel was raised, to give up a solid job, so he pressed the send button.

"Jo-jo," Robert said. "Where you at, rube? It's almost four."

"I have this week off," Joseph said. Robert chortled in the phone, but Joseph continued anyway, "Didn't anyone tell you?"

"Off my ass, dude. You're working like everybody else. Where are you?"

Joseph's heart sank. From his chair he slid down onto the carpeted ground. "I'm serious, Robert. I have this week off. Mike said he'd take care of me. I'm in Minneapolis."

"Minneapolis? You're fucking kidding me."

"No. Mike gave me these weeks off back in October. He said he'd take care of me." It seemed airtight to say so. Joseph could give the time and place where Mike said the words. A driver named Clyde and a driver named Phil sat in the communal area where the drivers gathered after their shift. They were showing each other the Lemon Party meme on their phones and Mike was putting a file away in his office. He wore tan slacks that day and a Hawaiian shirt. He drank a Mountain Dew.

"Oh my God," Robert said. "Hold on. You have to call Mike." Then Robert was gone, and before Joseph could find the courage to make the call, he had another.

"The fuck are you doing, Joseph? You're in fucking Minneapolis?"

"Mike, I don't understand, you said I had this time off."

"Hold the fucking phone, Joseph. I said we'd talk about it. This is peak season, everyone has to be here. You'd better get the fuck back here, like now."

"I can't get back, my flight for home leaves in an hour."

"Cool, Joseph, if you can't get here in the next twenty minutes, I'll have your termination papers ready for you when you do."

And Joseph was suddenly very fired up. "Okay, you do that, Mike."

"Will do, Jo, thanks for working with us." And Mike hung up.

After a few minutes, once the adrenaline waned and Joseph no longer felt like he could run through a brick wall, he started to wonder if a Bethel had ever been fired. Maybe this was how everyone got fired. All of it was one big setup. His phone buzzed. Robert again.

"Listen Joseph, you work at a good company. It could have a future for you. Don't throw it away. Let me talk to Mike, and when you get home, call us again."

In his solitary alcove, Joseph turned over the events of his possible future life. Jennifer worked with the non-profit that built houses, and what must it be like to use your hands, to build and do something good instead of being a prop in a gas-guzzling machine. All of a sudden Joseph dreamed dreams. He tried not to get into specifics, only telling Jennifer there was a "mix-up" at work and he was exploring his options.

"So what do you think?" Joseph spoke as if he actually would do it. "You think I could work with you for a couple months?"

"Yes," she said. "That'd be amazing!"

"Okay, I'll call my bosses here. It's kind of a mess."

"Now boarding, section three, now boarding section three." Joseph had to say goodbye. So he did, and when he landed in Sioux Falls, he called Harriet in Seattle.

"Get a flight back as soon as you can," Harriet said. "And call us tomorrow morning. We're going to discuss everything that's happened. You understand?"

"Okay," Joseph said, as if he had not talked to Jennifer at all.

Joseph's family came to greet him, and while these reunions would become less eventful in the coming years, that year everyone showed up: Mom and Dad, Joseph's sisters and their husbands and small children. The two little boys and the two little girls had made colorful signs with construction paper, written in their scrawled elementary handwriting, using pencils as poles, holding them up for everyone to see as the passengers walked through the glass doors of the humble security gate of the Sioux Falls airport. And when Joseph saw the signs, they held them even higher.

In their sedans, they all went to Joseph's oldest sister's place for a meal. How happy everyone was, eating their food and talking about their lives over the last year. Joseph thought about how many mistakes he'd made, adding little, and afterward rode home with his parents to Hudder, the town where he grew up. The next morning he went to the basement junk room with the cement floor, exposed 2x4s and a freezer full of meat, the pencil sharpener screwed into the wall. It was the only place in the house Dad allowed something like that. Joseph was on speakerphone. He heard their voices, hollow and echoing.

"...All right," Harriet said. "Now we need you to explain your side."

"Joseph," Mike interjected. "No matter what you think you heard, you should not expect to get these days off. Even if

I did say you were taken care of, which I did not, you should've verified the vacation with your new boss, Harriet."

Joseph tried to speak up again, but Mike said, "Understand how this works, buddy. If you ever want to move up, you're going to have to become more responsible. What are you doing now? You're away during our busiest time? That's not something someone who is serious about their career would do."

Mike was out in Seattle, standing in the middle of that office, dressed in a dark robe, and both Robert and Harriet had been placed on strategic podiums in the room, like in a séance. Joseph could see them.

"Now when you get back," Harriet said, sounding like a mother trying to quell an argument, "we'll have another meeting on this, and it's all going to go on your record. Okay, Joseph?"

"Okay," Joseph said, then said it again because he knew nothing else to say. "Okay."

Walking a few steps to another room, he tossed his phone onto his childhood bed. Fate had shown him a way out but he did not have the balls to take it. So, with the trip shortened that year, Joseph saw his grandpa and grandma only once and Grandpa Bethel hardly recognized his grandson. It made Joseph wish, harder than ever before, he could show his family he was not alone. Seeing everyone laughing and hugging significant others and eating familiar foods—little weenies and caramel popcorn and cracker dip made of half-cheese half-egg with jalapeño peppers—wore on him more than ever. That kind of feeling would get worse in coming years, until it stopped entirely, when Joseph and everyone else ceased to hope for something good to happen.

20

This was the plan before everything got bungled over Christmas. Joseph secretly drew up the idea to see Bethany in Minnesota. She lived eight hours away, and most of that drive would be straight north by way of a highway just blocks from his parent's house. Where she lived in that small northern town, Joseph had no clue, only that if he went, he might be able to make things right. But, with the trip home cut in half, there was no time. All the family activities, previously planned over two weeks, had been scrunched down to days.

In college, Joseph drove to Rapid City to see a girl he barely knew. Later, he pined for Mary Hutton for years. Not to mention flying to Alabama in the hopes that he could live with a sculptor he met on MySpace. None of those trips, those of the heart or those encompassing actual physical distance, worked, so it is unlikely Bethany would've fallen for such a quixotic gesture, but still Joseph cannot help but wonder things like,

"What if Mike had not been my boss? What if a more forgiving and amenable type like Harriet was in charge? Or better yet, what if I had just quit and gone up to see Bethany?"

Her absence began to weigh on him more heavily, and Joseph saw how he aged. More rapidly, then seemingly all at once. The hair on the top of his head began thinning as new grays emerged on the sides. Darkening patches formed under his eyes, and his face bulged. His chin sagged. Not for much longer could he depend on boyish looks. Just when he realized he wanted to rely on them, they began to fade. Still there were parties every weekend at the house of women, and after the drinking and playing of card games and singing of songs, Joseph would find himself with Jennifer. It started with retiring to the upstairs couch, and there she rubbed his head as he passed out. As time went along they moved under her shirt and below his belt, then to fewer clothes on either of them on the downstairs couch, and finally to her bed. And while Joseph thought he did a good job of keeping it quiet, Boris, Laurel's boyfriend, who worked at Boeing and parted his hair down the middle, heard the noises.

Drunk in the downstairs party room, both Boris and Joseph slumped on the wraparound couch with the residue of the evening—bottles and clothes and plastic guitars and drums—around them. They had done what they often did then: drank and stripped if they didn't get a high enough score on the game. That kind of thing was fun for about a year, until everyone got married or moved away to the suburbs or both.

"I just can't help it," Joseph was saying, his lap covered with a pillow. Boris wore boxers. "It's a mistake." Joseph hesitated, then said, "I think...I think I had a good thing with Bethany. I know that's dumb to say after she's gone, but it's true. I really screwed up."

"Bethany is beautiful," Boris said, which Joseph found odd because usually when referring to an attractive woman Boris used the word "hot."

"She is. I mean, I don't know why things ended. A bunch of dumb stuff...I have no idea."

"Bethany is beautiful," Boris said again, and in the early-morning bleary silence, she was, but nothing could be gained from knowing that.

Spring came, and the house of women entertained the group at their first barbecue. A halcyon day, Bethany was coming, so Joseph decided to go. He ate chips with hummus and tofu hot dogs in the backyard. All the new house builders came, young people just out of private universities with liberal viewpoints, some sitting in trees, blending into the greenery with their natural hair and smells. Inside in the calm living room facing the street, Joseph picked up a newspaper and pretended to read. Everything would be okay. All he needed was to see her. If he could see her, she'd understand.

A car pulled up to the driveway. Joseph walked along the wall until he got to the curtain. He hid there, watching as Bethany unloaded satchels from her green station wagon beside a man, a boy really, who gathered more. Joseph mindlessly walked back until he reached the chair and slithered down into it. His pores opened up and his words for her blurred. In the kitchen her familiar voice could be heard talking with someone about Bellingham. Joseph peeked one eye over the paper. Just as he did, Bethany looked into the living room. Quickly Joseph flipped the paper back up, but she saw. Soft approaching footsteps over the carpeted floor. Once she was close enough, he pulled down the paper, as if he had just finished reading a fascinating article.

"Joseph," Bethany said, offering a small wave, similar to the one when they first met.

"Bethany, hey. Didn't know you were coming." It pained him, how trim and fit she looked. "How's school going?"

"Good, good," she said. "I'm getting to know some people finally, so that's good."

"Nice," Joseph said, fully aware the magic words he'd planned to give her had dissolved into vapor. "Did you get something to eat?"

"I haven't," she said. "Did you?"

"I did, real good, full." And he patted his belly, so they had a brief, forced laugh, then they spoke at the same time. "It's beau—" Joseph said, while Bethany said, "Well, I'm..."

"...Sorry," Bethany said. "What was that?"

"Oh, nothing. I was just going to say how nice it is outside, but you should go get something to eat, Bethany. You're wasting away."

That made her smile, Joseph thought wistfully, like the time they said goodbye under Bruce, but it was more like the smile someone gives when they feel sorry for someone else. "I'll see you out there then?" she asked.

"Oh yes. Yes, yes." Joseph had longed to see Bethany, starved for months to see her, but he said nothing more.

Maybe an hour later in the small backyard, the sun going down over the wooden fence, and Bethany held hands with her boy as they talked with Tina. Joseph could not hear them. He just stared at the guy's hippie sandals. Then came a dousing of warm water, like a waterfall in his belly, as he watched Bethany tousle his surfer-blond hair. The back door right behind him, Joseph twirled and went through it, taking a small pause in the open kitchen—as if he had gone in there to fetch something—then kept walking, first to the front door, and out of the house.

21

The second summer in the city became a mild one, temperate enough to be the main thing Joseph reported back to Dad when asked what "the big news" was. No full-time job or significant relationship leading to marriage, nothing like that, the only news to report centered around the weather. Work on the boats started up again, but it didn't seem right to Joseph to be back there, as if he were taping over the film of his dreams, somehow erasing a true calling he could not quite make out. In those times, the builders, hippies, and the house of women played Frisbee in the park. They called it Ultimate, and even after more than a year in the city Joseph treasured being included. He would've killed for such an opportunity in Sioux Falls, to be in an adult sports league, so as to show others he could be an athlete. Because of the game, Joseph saw Bethany for the second time that year. Their only correspondence had been an exchange of emails after the barbecue wherein Joseph apologized for being aloof.

"I'm sorry, too," Bethany wrote in response. "I didn't know how to act in front of you." Did she have residual feelings? Joseph read on. "But, as you know, I've started my life up here and I think it's best if we keep being friends. Hope all is well. Bye, buddy."

To forget, Joseph hung out with William that summer when the sun shined every day. William's girlfriend, lying out by the field, a towel beneath her, wearing a sunflower hat and a bikini bottom, while William, long and wiry, jumped as high as a basketball player for the Frisbee, scoring more than anyone else. Beverly, a new house builder, played as well. Joseph knew her name and where she was from, somewhere in the South.

"You should talk to her for sure," William said to Joseph on the sidelines. "She's got a nice bubble butt."

They laughed together, though Joseph inwardly pined for her crushingly well-proportioned and athletic backside, flexing in her short shorts. When he got the chance, he guarded Beverly closely, and every time his team scored he took the opportunity to tell her the score. She had straight brown hair and a button-like face, and after the game that day they sat Indian-style under a small apple tree on the grass. They pulled blades from the ground, placing the strands on each other's legs while William recovered with his girlfriend, napping in the sun. When they woke, William lazily strolled over.

"We're heading out," William said, his girlfriend's face obscured by her large sun hat. "But we thought we might head to Golden Gardens. You guys wanna come?"

"Sounds great," Beverly said immediately. That was that.

On the way to the beach, Joseph sang along in his car to a pop song. It made Beverly giggly, in a conspicuous manner, and he thought, by the way she covered her mouth, that she would not mention this to anyone. At the beach, William had set up a small grill. They drank beer and ate hot dogs and burgers. Joseph buried Beverly's feet in the sand, and it seemed to please her, but he could not stop thinking about his parking spot. Not quite right, he thought, too close to other cars, and so he drifted to nightmare scenarios of dents and the end of the world.

Just days before on the way to William's, Joseph drove too close to a cement barrier while merging onto the University Bridge—because he was too aware of other cars—and that in turn pushed him into the barrier. Seeing his reflection in Beverly's round sunglasses, Joseph wanted to forget all that. Her cleavage, gently baking in the sun, made him aware of his testicles and penis, how he might get to touch her body soon enough, and he drifted off to the business of the beach. Far-off babble of children playing, college girls in bikinis playing volleyball, the smell of salt water washing up on the shore. The world did not care about anything he had ever done, and they packed up when the day got cooler. William and his girlfriend went to their apartment as Joseph left with Beverly.

"So what's next?" she asked as they drove. There was a movie theater close to her shared house, a block from Bethany's old bike shop, so that's what they decided to do. Joseph waited on her porch, thanking God for an empty space to park, and soon Beverly came down, her face pink from the day. They walked to the nearby movie theater, holding hands for the first time as the theater went dark. After, in her room, Beverly put on music from her computer. There was a stand-up mirror, positioned in such a way that Joseph could watch as she moved up and down on him. She made such small noises.

Finished, Joseph lay beside Beverly on her clean sheets, and he boasted to himself that he was one who, at that point in the history of all mankind, could admire Beverly's pair of fading-pink boy shorts. She wore no bra, her teardrops against him, and he thought how lucky he was to have ended up where he'd ended up. His car was parked blocks away, and in the next moment an intense fear struck him. He may not have parked right and could cause an accident. In the street, only death.

22

William and his girlfriend went off to graduate school in Chicago and Madison, cities near home in Indiana and Wisconsin. In that time Joseph considered applying for graduate school, as his mom encouraged him to, but when Joseph began to organize the work—retaining letters of recommendation, taking entrance exams, sending in fees—he just as soon dropped the idea. Instead, he kept doing the same thing: sleeping, working at jobs, eating frozen foods. He golfed on the weekends with Boris, and drank at the house of women. It would seem an all right life, comfortable, if not for the continual erosion of his mind.

Micah moved back to Seattle from Austin, where he had lived with Polly. One night after returning, he attended a service at Church of the Wanderers called The Circle, an arts event where painters painted as poets recited poetry and musicians played folk music. Micah went because a friend was going to play guitar, though as Micah explained to Joseph over the phone, he left after getting a "touchy-feely vibe." They talked about it in Joseph's bedroom, which hardly fit them both, regardless of the number of square feet.

"Those fucking reptiles," Micah was saying. "That's what those fuckers are, goddamn reptiles, passing around scraps of paper and everyone was 'encouraged' to write down their feelings and put them in the basket. Oh yeah, with your fucking telephone number and email address. What the fuck, man."

"Yeah man, that place is messed up." Joseph said the word "man" in Micah's presence much more than he did in any other context.

"Shit, and I have some other news," Micah said, his head lowering. "Polly and I are done."

Finally, Joseph thought. Micah always wanted to be with other women. "So you're a free man now?" Joseph asked.

But Micah must not have heard, and he said, jealousy bubbling in his voice, "I am telling you right now, Joseph. I am demonstratively sure Polly's cunt friend put her up to this. She's always pulling this drama bullshit. I know she resents me and my politics and I'm fucking sure she's trying to get back at me in her own snide way. Joseph, this is the shit I'm talking about, man. Polly wanted us to be grownups and this is the childish shit I have to put up with, 'breaking up'? You know, I have incriminating photos of her. I'm not talking about PG-13 shit, either…well, I'm not going to get into it, but I could sell that shit. Man, I look back at it, and I can see how much of a child Polly was, is, how sycophantic. She wanted someone she could ride, and now that I'm not hot shit, she wants something else. Fucking cunt."

Joseph said nothing, seemingly no reward in risking the wrong response. But the silence disappointed Micah, his eyes turning more sad than vengeful.

"Come on, man. You're with me, right?"

"Of course," Joseph said quickly. "Sorry. Just sounds like a tough situation. I really am sorry, man. Did you still want to go out?" Joseph only asked this halfheartedly.

"Man," Micah said. "I don't know. Did you want to?"

"Only if you want to. You're probably not feeling the best."

"You're right, man, maybe I'll just head out." Micah said he'd be staying with a friend in another part of the city, and Joseph was so relieved by that fact, that night, he had his best sleep in months. Micah called a few days later, asking for tips on how to "get bitches on the internet," and Joseph gave advice, tips he thought Micah already knew about what they both, back in their evangelical days, would have called the courtship process. The awkward conversation was over.

"So what's this new number you're calling from?" Joseph asked.

"Yeah, guess which bitch did that." Micah went on to explain how Polly stopped paying his phone bill. Joseph wished he hadn't asked, and, as he hung up, had the thought that they would never talk again.

At that juncture in his life, Joseph sensed himself further away from where he wanted to be than ever before. His classmates in Hudder had, by then, married and begun prospering in farming or business. Sleeping with Jennifer helped, but the temporary comfort that brought was short-lived and followed by grave regret. So he had trysts. One from the internet was taller than he was, almost six foot two, and worked for the Seattle Library. They ate pho and went to her place, a dome by a lake in Renton, where they watched a movie and smoked weed—first time for Joseph—and he slept over. Nothing happened in the evening but in the morning the stranger asked, "Do you want me to suck your cock?" Joseph said yes and she went to it like a chore. The biggest event in that time was when he got rejected for the full-time pool at the package delivery company.

"You're just not ready," Harriet told Joseph that day in her office, harsh fluorescent light above them. "I have some things you can work on, though. Start taking clearer notes. And talk slower on the phone. You talk so fast I can hardly understand you. Also, the way you staple the reports together, it seems like you're doing it haphazardly on purpose. Let's clean those things up, and you'll be on your way."

Joseph would have to wait six months to try again, a fact he did not share with Dad. Instead Joseph relayed, "Well, with the economy the way it is, the company just isn't hiring full-time employees." As for the rest of that fall, nothing happened, and it became a lost season, along with the others that have accumulated for Joseph Bethel.

Winter, and the unlikely snow made navigating the steep streets of the city challenging. Hipsters welcomed the season like schoolchildren. They fashioned sleds from the lids of garbage cans and cardboard boxes from Apple products and slid down the hills of their neighborhood. All of them in tight pants and loose scarves and colorful knit hats, proclaiming it was "the way it should be." Of course, their beer, shelter, and entertainment were brought to them by large trucks with giant tires and smoky exhausts driving in good weather. No one talked about this. Across the city, not just up in arty neighborhoods, traffic had been put to a halt, so when Joseph walked to work he saw remnants of tire chains on the frozen residential streets, though he never did spot a plow. Rumor had it Seattle owned only one, which felt true, even if it wasn't.

The reason Joseph walked to work was that driving risked an accident. By then, the dent had embedded deep in his mind, living there, interrupted only by the occasional lust-filled aspiration of someone new. He had called the man with the dog again, but it once more went to voice mail. Joseph let the nothingness continue to rot inside him. And there was the problem of the ever-inflating tire of fat around his waist. Office work with pizza for lunch and donuts for breakfast, along with drinking at night, made his face bigger. If he just could get back to the streamlined, taut version he moved to Seattle with, he believed, the one that attracted Bethany, things could go in the right direction. There was no controlling the hairs falling out of the top of his head, the darkening circles under his eyes, but he could control his belly. Walking would do some good.

The largest of the snows came over a weekend in December, and on the Monday after it still came down. Peering out the bay window of the Substance living room, Joseph sensed the ten-mile walk in front of him, its length and accompanying frigidity. But there would be no such thing as not making it to work. If he got bundled up now, he'd show up on time in the early afternoon. So Joseph put on two pairs of white long socks, long johns, khaki work pants, an undershirt, then over that a button-down, along with a hooded sweatshirt and a blue-and-red stocking hat. Like a snowman, he put his hands in his pockets, said goodbye to the warm ones in the Substance living room, and took off. The snow was delicate, and from time to time Joseph slipped, as he wore dress shoes, not wanting to lug a bag along with him. Cars stuck on the side of the road made him glad he had not risked the highway or interstate, though he knew he knew how to drive, he just doubted he could, which bothered him much more. At work, drivers loitered in the office, giving off the air of a school day being cut short.

"It was hell out there," several said, though it would get worse over the next weeks, packages piling up in the warehouse, causing management on top of management to run around on top of each other, saying things to those below them which made no difference at all.

When the last driver returned, Joseph got bundled up and headed out into the industrial area, planning to walk all the way back again, when a Good Samaritan appeared. It could have been that he saw Joseph biff it on the barren, icy road and slowed down in his station wagon, which looked much like Bethany's, because he felt bad. Whatever it was, Joseph felt very thankful, and responded by not hesitating to get in after receiving the offer. Inside the cold car, the man wore a husky toughness, a dirty face and an even dirtier leather coat, but put Joseph at ease when he said, "So a hired slave over there, huh," as if everyone already knew about Mike.

He drove them down the desolate road, pacing the vehicle's every move, seemingly aware of every rotation of the tires. Downtown, he had to go the other way, so with a wave and another thank-you Joseph took off on foot in the brightly lit International District, wearing slippery dress shoes. He called Laurel from his flip phone. When she answered, her voice was warm like honey, and it reminded Joseph of a utopian time when he first came to Seattle. He wanted to be where Laurel was, all snug. The picture she gave with her voice was so vivid, he could practically see her huddled up on the couch, drinking hot chocolate. She guided Joseph to the right bus stop, and there he found a mass of cold-bruised people. Taking up with the shivering group, he waited a half hour. To pass the time, he thought about the beginning, Laurel's convulsive orgasms, and as the trance went deeper their ebullience shined a rainbow through his dark winter. When the bus came like a ship of hope, the sight was met with loud murmurs and audible hoorays. As it opened its retractable doors, all the people greedily got on. With no seats available, Joseph stood, immediately overhearing a conversation between a middle-aged lady and two young women. They went back and forth about the weather.

"Back home, this never happens," the middle-aged lady was saying, sounding as though she had been driving home her point for a good several stops. "We can drive through a little snow. It's awful this whole city would shut down from this."

Out of nowhere, a young woman answered, "I'm from South Dakota. I know…"

"Like I said," the middle-aged lady interrupted. "I'm from Ohio and it shouldn't be like this." She went on from there about how it should be until the next stop, where she got off, along with a fair amount of others. Their parting made room in front of the young woman from South Dakota, who sat with another. Joseph never approached strangers, but the fierceness of the conditions emboldened him.

"I agree with you," he said as he turned. "Ohio doesn't have mountains like they do close to Seattle. I'm from South Dakota, by the way." And he reached out his hand.

Wearing sensible winter gear, they smiled back in sisterly union, as that is what they were, and with the bus driver caring for their safety, they got to know each other. The South Dakotans came from Arlington, SD, and it impressed them both that Joseph would know their school's mascot (Cardinals). The prettier of the two wore red earrings and had straight hair the color of cinnamon, flowing out of her stocking hat. Joseph imagined a farmer in South Dakota called her "Princess." Before getting off the bus, he managed to secure their phone numbers. What divine goodness the storm had been. Walking the rest of the blocks to the house of women, Joseph again had hope.

At home for the holidays that year, vacation cleared in advance, Joseph sat in front of his parents' computer and read Seattle newspapers online. The front pages told stories of citizens not getting their Christmas presents, showing a picture of a driver Joseph personally knew delivering in the elements. It was good to be home, the children of Joseph's cousins and sisters grew like weeds, and Mom, because it is what she always does no matter how old her son gets, told Joseph how handsome he was. Joseph and Dad talked sports, as well as the pending full-time job at the package delivery company. One of the last nights, they watched Old Yeller. As they did, Joseph imagined Bethany resting her head on his shoulder, eating the caramel popcorn Mom made, laughing her big happy laugh, as Dad sang the Old Yeller song one more time. But Joseph was alone, pushing toward the end of his twenties. No one mentioned his singleness, instead they focused on the small children and their needs, be it a slice of cheese or a piece of cake or a toy. Once over the holiday Joseph corresponded with Jennifer, though it was just sending nude pictures to one another. When he got back to Seattle, he called the sisters from South Dakota, but the date resulted in a disappointingly boring dinner, instead of a thrilling threesome.

Joseph met Jia from the internet soon after, going to a movie where she wore heels and a black coat that covered her from her neck to her knees—making it seem like she wore nothing else—and at her apartment with wood floors, in her bedroom, Joseph found himself taking off her black stockings. Then, as he ran his hands up her thighs, to the outcropping of her ass, he had the distinct notion of knowing he never felt anything so supple. In the morning he woke to the sound of Jia blow-drying her hair. He got up and went to the noise. She stood in the bathroom in a silk flowered dress. It barely covered her, and Joseph wanted to take it off, but he knew, by the way she'd restlessly moved after they finished the night before, she did not want any part of him again.

"I should go," Joseph said, to which Jia agreed with a friendly hug goodbye. On the way to Substance, Joseph entertained the idea that the dent had something to do with why he didn't properly move her in bed. Whatever the case, Jia's embarrassed eyes stayed with him.

Isabella Garcia and Joseph bonded over YouTube videos. She knew about the funny ones that advertised unneeded, commercial things like blanket pajamas. On their first date they went to a bar, and Isabella arrived late with black-dyed hair, a small piercing through her nose, and a body hidden by a tweed coat. At some point, Joseph asked about movies, about which ones Isabella had seen and not seen.

"We could watch it tonight?" he asked under purple neon lights, cozy in the back by the jukebox.

"Okay," Isabella said, her black bangs falling over her eyes. "But you have to promise not to be an ax killer, okay?" Joseph agreed and paid for the drinks.

"I like when I know people can hear me," Isabella said in her bedroom, opening the window. It never ceased to amaze him, the different things that people did.

The next weekend, Joseph at her place again, they put in a scary movie and Isabella lit her bong. On the couch, she took off his jeans, and Joseph was glad, as she had very sensual lips and gave head in a way that made his penis disappear.

Only once did Isabella go to Substance, and the morning after, as Joseph woke next to her brown body, they could hear his roommates out in the kitchen. Isabella hid her head in the pillow.

"They won't care," Joseph said, kissing Isabella's hair, which smelled of smoke. "I'm serious. They won't."

It convinced her enough that they got dressed and went through the kitchen where his roommates formed a gauntlet, each of them giving staggered good-mornings. Her hair sprouting everywhere, Isabella only nodded, and Joseph said hello for the both of them. On the street, holding hands was little comfort for Isabella, who kept saying over and over on the drive back, "God that was awful." They saw each other once more after that, splitting amicably for no reason at all.

The next was Allison Pushay. "Yes, I was teased," she remarked to Joseph. Allison worked with the League of Women Voters, grew up with two journalist parents in Montana, and, as Joseph found in her Capitol Hill studio apartment, kept stacks of books on her floor and in rows on several bookcases. Their first date was at a bar, the one down the street where Joseph met Isabella. Though, unlike Isabella, Allison looked little like her pictures. Instead of the petite, large-eyed girl online, she was bigger and broader, like she could play as a tight end in football, with lots of blond hair and tattoos on her arms.

For a month they saw each other, and Joseph was always happy to, as Allison said things he had always wanted to hear, texting him, "I want you to fuck me in my ass." He was still an inexperienced lover, compared to others his age, so when Joseph would hear Allison say in person, "Do you want it like this?" and do it just like he told her to, it pleased him endlessly. One morning, the creeping light of dawn teasing the sky, the rain tapping on the roof of Substance, Joseph's tired arm draped over Allison's naked breasts. He started to drift back to sleep, content to have someone as womanly as her, when he heard, like out of a dream, "How do I know you don't have AIDS?"

Joseph looked up. Allison was staring at him. Stuttering, he did not know what to say. He'd always assumed he would never have more than one partner.

"You don't," Joseph said, closing his eyes but sensing she was still looking at him. They stayed awake, restless, apparently sure that would be the last time for them, and it was.

23

The house, sandwiched amongst a row of other modest-look-ing but in fact very expensive houses—considering their loca-tion—going down the east side of Wallingford Avenue near 40th Street, only blocks from where Bethany once lived, is where Joseph began to go to suck out its youthful manna. Just being inside could revive his sagging skin and retreating hair. Once upon a time Joseph Bethel believed himself handsome, all the way up until he moved to Seattle. But as he reached his thirties, he began to think he had skipped a few years. The mild aging of his early twenties had gone ahead to the harsh and steep changes of someone else's early forties. Looking at pictures taken before Seattle, ones snapped at a party his fam-ily threw for him in Sioux Falls, it seemed as though the world waited for him to conquer it, his hair black and flopped over the forehead. Just a couple years later, Joseph's hair had grayed, and he combed it in a very specific way so as to not look very bald.

The ones from the house, "the Cool House," a name coined by Boris, would help. Joseph met them by way of the Frisbee games in Wallingford Park, Richard Updike and Tommy Bleary. Fresh out of college in North Carolina, both had made the first big move to Seattle. Tommy, whose sister worked with Jennifer and Tina building houses, introduced himself first, giving Joseph a cautious handshake as they put on their cleats before a game. And from that very first handshake, the way he looked him up and down, Joseph sensed Tommy checking to see if "this guy" would be hitting on his little sister. Richard welcomed Joseph with less eyeballing, laughing more when Joseph made a joke about their college, which had an admissions commercial that went "Hot. hot. hot. Hot. Hot. Hot. Appalachian is hot hot HOT!" That day started them, but their galvanizing came on Valentine's Day. Tommy enjoyed organizing parties just as much as he liked meeting little old ladies at grocery stores or getting cheap deals at auctions online for things like big-screen televisions he would never use. Tommy Bleary was type A, talked with a drawl, and often called Joseph "buddy."

"You gotta come on over, buddy. Wear your best suit, too. We're going to dress up and go downtown. It'll be the anti–Valentine's Day kind of day."

So Joseph went to the Cool House, its walls thick with hot people falling over each other with careless post-college abandon, not one of them worrying about a bad-hair day or gaining weight, walking through its doors wearing his dressiest combo.

Not a suit, since Joseph did not have a job where he needed to wear one, and that bothered him earlier in the evening as he went to his closet to get dressed, and especially so as he saw the rest in their secondhand wares bought from consignment stores. How comfortably they fit on their slim bodies. For the first time since moving to Seattle, Joseph stuck out as the oldest. Tommy encouraged him anyway.

"You look good, buddy," Tommy said in the kitchen smelling vaguely of weed and more distinctly of the buttered noodles being stirred in a large pot. Maybe, Joseph thought, he could be the man of the group. Hand out wise advice.

They went by bus downtown, starting the bar crawl at the top of a hotel where they drank mixed drinks. Joseph found himself buffered by two literary types, Richard Updike and Richard's friend, Caroline Moore, a poet. A pale woman in her late twenties with a severe face, mentioning that she wrote every day using a typewriter.

"You don't feel good if I don't write, do you?" she asked Richard, as if it were a bodily function which must be expunged. Richard agreed, though it all went over Joseph's head.

Still he hung tight, alluding to a nonexistent well of information as Richard and Caroline discussed modern novels, which apparently came in the form of something called a chapbook, a term Joseph had never heard. Clueless or not, Joseph liked that Richard and Caroline did not seem as young as the rest at the hotel bar, many of whom seemed closer to high school. After the hotel, they went street level a little tipsy. One of the revelers in another pack within the group wore all black: shoes, stockings, and a short dress. It was a fool's errand, but

Joseph kept tabs on her, and at the last bar of the night, he sat across from her. Her name was Vanessa. She was born in Puerto Rico but grew up in Manhattan. She was right there.

"I have something to tell you," Joseph slurred, his ninth and last drink almost gone. "But I can't tell you here. The only way I could ever tell you is if I called you."

"But then I'd have to give you my number." And Vanessa did. She wrote it down on a coaster with a pen she pulled from her discreet, black purse.

On the way home in the bus, Joseph caught a glimpse of himself in the window. Maybe it was the alcohol blurring his mind, but he was sure he saw someone who could still have everything he ever wanted.

The next day, fighting off the blues of a Sunday night, Joseph watched a television show with Boris and Laurel and Jennifer at the house of women, all of them on one couch, scrunched together and "getting tight," as Boris liked to say. The two women had a tendency to fall asleep, so Boris liked to play the game of putting his hand in front of their faces when their eyes closed. It was happening again that night. With the humorous distraction, Joseph was free to look at his phone, buzzing under the blanket.

"Hi," it said with a smiley face. Vanessa. Soon, Joseph thought, there would be a better job. The dent, it seemed impossible that it would always be on his mind. And he could work on his body.

So they went for pho that week, and Joseph noticed across from her what he had not noticed at the bar, Vanessa's tar-colored freckles splattered across her exquisitely molded face.

He loved them. She did not wear anything revealing, not like on Valentine's Day, and that seemed to embolden him even more, that she was not so cosmopolitan. Vanessa could be the next Bethany. Afterward, on the drive to her downtown loft, one she shared with a couple, Vanessa name-dropped an Olympic gold-medal swimmer, saying they used to hang out in Michigan. But Joseph did not worry, lunch had gone so well, and before Vanessa left his car he gave her a peck on the cheek. Three days later, a reply to his offer of another date.

"I've been sick this week, sorry," Vanessa wrote, even adding a frowning face emoticon. Joseph texted back, but he never heard from her again.

24

Others, always there would be others, at houses with drinking games and early-afternoon brunches. Richard lived at the newest and most promising one. He once had been a creative writing major in college. There were tattoos on his shoulders, and he wanted to be a novelist. That intrigued Joseph, and soon enough they became good friends. Tommy still called others douche and faggot and played tackle football and often drank until six in the morning. Richard was a little older and had stories about writers, how they found it tough to get going in the world of literature. Joseph identified with them, even if he was not a writer. In that time at a party, Richard introduced Joseph to Heidi. She worked at the same pizza place as Caroline. On a Friday night, Joseph in the house with loud music and breasts and asses all rubbing into each other. The hot alcohol went down throats. Fresh faces moved about, their whisked-over thick hair and bangs becoming sweaty. Later, Joseph in the kitchen with Heidi, her tongue stained black from wine. She boasted a long-limbed body, her face showing a few scars from pimples, long ago. She talked about how she once wrote stories too.

"After Caroline read my last one, she gave it back to me and just told me to 'keep writing.'" And they both laughed, knowing how Caroline could be about, as she called it, "the holy craft." Electronic music played in the living room. Heidi then leaned in toward Joseph's ear and said, "So are we going to make out, or what?"

They put down their drinks and went to the backyard, grabbing each other before they planted themselves underneath a plum tree. Heidi straddled Joseph on a plastic lawn chair, and they moved down to the ground. Fruit burst underneath them. She unzipped his jeans in the mud.

"I love your cock," she said, and soon he finished inside her mouth. Heidi went inside laughing, with Joseph beaming and trying to compose himself. After he slipped in the back of the Cool House, sitting down with what remained of the party, Caroline seemed to be the only one cogent enough to ask any questions.

"Why are your jeans so dirty? What's on your shirt? What were you two doing?"

Everyone else, too high or too drunk or both, just thought the questions were hilarious.

A reading, organized by Richard, came soon after the night with Heidi, and the one Joseph hoped to see was Ali Claremont, another house builder and best friend to Alexandra. Alexandra, with giant breasts but a small waist—one Joseph could have put his hands around and touched his fingers—lived at the Cool House with others: Tommy and sometimes his long-term long-distance girlfriend in San Francisco, Polly and George in a room downstairs, and Tommy's sister, who saw different men.

Ali, though, it was Ali who would fix everything in Joseph's life. She hailed from Chicago and visited the Cool House and Jim's as well, the cheap beer joint all the house builders liked. Joseph rarely went to Jim's, not wanting to risk seeing Bethany, who showed up on occasion with her new boyfriend, Jeff, not the surfer with blond hair, but another who also worked building houses. But one Saturday night, Joseph did go and happened to see Ali. In the back of the moldy bar, she and others played pool. Her wavy hair, crooked smile, and starry eyes, Joseph loved everything about her, even the faint yellow cakes of plaque on her bottom teeth and hair sprouting in her armpits. Joseph knew how square he looked in comparison to her, in his collared shirt and neat jeans. All he could do was take account of Ali as much as one takes account of the most attractive person in a group.

Beer pong and flip cup set events in motion. They all played one night at the Cool House—the same night that Richard and Caroline made a pact to one day move to Eastern Washington and start a writing commune—and at the end, Ali milled in the kitchen with Joseph.

"It's really boring," Joseph said about his job. "You don't want to hear about it, Ali. Seriously."

"Oh, but it's sexy, I think. Don't you wear the little shorts?" And Ali rubbed at Joseph's legs where the cuffs would end.

"It's not quite like that," Joseph said. "I'm in an office." And that deflated Ali, Joseph could see by the way she retracted her hand, though a small quiver returned to her lips as he clarified that he was a boss of the ones who wore the shorts. As for Ali's work, there was little to tell. She worked where Bethany had, Beverly, and Jennifer too.

By the end of the night, before Joseph slept on one of the many Cool House couches, he acquired Ali's number, and in the days that followed they texted. Joseph hinted that they should see each other somewhere other than the Cool House, and Ali was always fast with responses. Things like "You're really something, Joseph Bethel," and "I just don't know about you."

Sooner than later, they had a date, which meant Joseph needed to drive to her, which was a problem. Someone would die because of him, of that he was sure. His tires would fall off and his insurance would never cover the damage and he would be in debt forever and all the work he put in at the package delivery company would go to paying for the problems his flying tires had caused. Nearing Ali's exit, Joseph almost had to stop and call to cancel. Pressing on, thinking of the night they exchanged numbers and made out, if only briefly, he arrived to Ali's rented house in West Seattle and parked far away so he would not have to be on a hill. It was the afternoon, halcyon in the spring, and Joseph wanted more than anything to think just of Ali and her wavy hair and hippie face and starry eyes. She welcomed him from the front porch.

"So good to see you," she said, and they hugged. She was warm and smelled like herbs. In her backyard, with chickens in a wire coop, she talked about her plans for grad school in Oregon, though more about one of her roommates.

"I'm serious, he can do anything," Ali said, taking a drag of her cigarette. "I think he's rock climbing today. God, he's fucking awesome." Joseph could see the man in his mind clearly. He was playing the bongos.

After a second cigarette, Ali and Joseph decided to go inside for a drink. It was then, with Cat Stevens playing, that things got better. In the backyard, Ali seemed to Joseph to have a thousand better things to do with a thousand more interesting people, but as "Hard Headed Woman" began to play and she finished her second glass, Joseph started to believe he was like any other guy who knew how to properly pack a bowl and run an urban farm.

"I'm so chill right now," Ali said, touching Joseph's knee. That was, apparently, all that was needed. That night, they slept together.

The following weekend, after a camping trip with Laurel and Boris and Jennifer, Joseph received a text message from Bob, Tina's man. As a man of few words, he sent, "Ali, huh?"

Joseph messaged back when they got out of the wilderness. "If you consider playing Scrabble something, then yes, Ali!"

But it was more than that, and Joseph hoped for that more as he went to Ali on a Friday. He stopped at a liquor store, splurging on a bottle of good wine, and from there called to tell Ali what he got.

"You get whatever you want, Joseph. I fucking love old wine, though. Italian wine, 'cause I'm Italian. Fucking love it."

So he went to her with the wine, though when she answered the door, Ali seemed to not know who it was that stood before her.

"You were actually coming over?" Ali slapped her forehead. "All right, I guess you wanna come in?" And she grandly gestured for Joseph to enter.

Ambient music pulsed through her place. Joseph brought Scrabble to where they played the last time, and they tried to re-create that evening, but this time it was sloppy, and before long they quit and listened to music in Ali's room, then they didn't do that either. Ali put a movie in her computer and began to take off her layers. On top of him, she took it out and pulled away.

"I'm sorry," Ali said, taking the covers and putting them over her. "I can't do this, I'm not like this." And she turned away and said to the wall, "You can stay over if you want."

Joseph did, because he thought it would be rude otherwise, but in the morning he left without saying goodbye. About a month later, at a rock concert with some members of the whole group, Joseph overheard Ali call him a "man-whore."

So she never came to the literary reading, but Tommy was there, along with twenty or so other people. They set up couches in the living room and put down rugs. Lit-friendly young people filled the place, some Joseph had never seen. The room smelled of incense as Caroline read a poem in a singsong style, using the word "milky" more than once. Her habit was to pull down her sheet of paper, then look up, seemingly to ask the audience in a wilting manner, "They aren't good, are they?" Her poems spun on an axis of lost love—not so secretly Richard—and elicited audible reactions after the most personal lines. Reading softly, rapidly, she went from one poem to the next, and when she stopped for good, she raised her hands, then put them back down again. A polite applause scattered the room.

Richard was next, sitting on a piano bench with his legs crossed. Torso hunched, foppish brown hair lapped over his brown-rimmed glasses, his short story mixed metaphor and autobiography, and everyone clapped, louder than for Caroline, when it was done. Joseph read after that, a "dumb thing," as he introduced it, he recently had put together. Tommy sat in the front row with his girlfriend from San Francisco and hollered after Joseph announced the title, as a spectator might at a rowdy football game. It wobbled Joseph, though he was sure Tommy did it because he believed a Midwesterner could handle such a thing, that only "fairies" couldn't take it.

Joseph read, and the crowd seemed to grow restless as it went on too long, but near the end, when he thought it picked up steam, a swell of adrenaline ran up his throat, and afterward Joseph received what he thought was a nice round of clapping. Then, as he walked out of the limelight, a poet friend of Caroline's, with a small, Yoko Ono-looking companion, said, "Wow." Though Joseph never did find out if it had been an inspired wow or an incredulous one, since his head was down in faux modesty.

Tommy read a rhyming poem last, and most there understood who and what it was about, Joseph and Maureen. Maureen, Alexandra's best friend, had come for a visit the weekend before. That Saturday night, after they all drank and danced, Joseph slept on their couch, and the next morning went with them to brunch on a sunny day, then to the beach at Golden Gardens. Through it all, Joseph sensed a closeness. Maureen, who wore an oversized Boston Celtics sweatshirt and a bikini bottom, talked with him longer than with the others, and they sat next to each other at brunch, and on the beach he covered her feet in sand. More and more throughout their time together, Joseph envisioned himself moving to a hamlet in Boston, because he thought that's what they were called in Boston, maybe getting a transfer with the package delivery company as Maureen finished her graduate school. Someday, if all went well and she inspired him to reach his potential, he might get into Harvard.

Though as Joseph listened to Tommy rhyme "you and me" with "other fish in the sea," then cringed from the bubbles of laughter crowding the room, he experienced two divergent branches of thought. One was simple and ended as soon as it came: Tommy's smirk was a show of brotherhood. They were equals in the war of the sexes. But the other led Joseph somewhere darker. It explained, not so subtly, how ridiculous it was for someone like Joseph to go after Maureen, someone more attractive than even Tommy's own girlfriend.

That thought path kept Joseph up that night, even after enough drinks to normally make him pass out. And it kept him up for nights and nights after that, and years and years, accompanied by another, more somber, thought: "I am going to be alone for the rest of my life."

25

Time passes. In the living room of the Cool House, Joseph is trying to get some sleep on the couch. He still went there, talking to those who'd listen about love and God and lost chances. On a weekend night, he had started to feel sick as soon as he arrived to the Halloween party. Over now, and those remaining had gone to knock on doors then run away before the owners answered. Joseph abandoned the group after a few doors and keenly felt, as the rest wore fewer clothes and he wore a fake college-professor getup, he should not have been there. He hoped to fall asleep soon, then it could all be like a dream.

Sometime in the dark morning, Joseph woke to rustling on the front porch. Tommy's voice and the voice of Marty, a fraternity buddy of Tommy's from North Carolina who always kept a dip in his mouth, along with Richard's voice, and the voices of two women. One was Linda, a tiny woman from

Long Island who wrote short stories, Richard's new girlfriend. The other was Marty's girlfriend. Joseph saw trails of cigarette smoke filter up toward the porch light. He wrapped himself tighter in the blanket, sweating beads, and knew if he could just fall asleep again, things might be okay. He scrunched further in the blanket. Unsure how much time had passed, he heard movement toward the door. Joseph put the blanket over his face at the expense of his toes.

"Tommy," Marty said as the door opened, "is that old dude going to be on the couch?"

"The fuck," Tommy yelled as they stormed in. He had worn a costume Joseph did not understand. "Get up, Joe, you can't sleep yet, buddy." He slapped at Joseph's feet.

"He's sleeping," Linda said, rolling her eyes. That's what Joseph remembers most of Linda, how often she did that.

"He's not fucking sleeping," Tommy said. "Joe, wake up." Richard was laughing. They all were. "We're going to party. Time to get up."

They went to the kitchen, then back into the dining room as they talked about the doors they'd knocked on. Marty wore a gorilla suit while his girlfriend wore tan trousers and a safari hat and carried a butterfly net. Someone ran over and put the net over Joseph's face.

"Come on," Tommy yelled from the dining room. "Get the fuck up, buddy, it's early."

"You old fuck, sleeping on that couch?" Marty said, and everyone laughed. "Get off the fucking couch."

"Wake up!" Tommy yelled.

"That's my couch," Marty said. "Gorilla needs couch."

They all were laughing heartily by the time Joseph took the net off his face. He envisioned them in the dining room looking good, rested, even in unforgiving, artificial light. How ridiculous to have come. His life had become a joke. Joseph swept off the blanket, dragging it along with him, and did not look at the others as he lay down on the last available couch, half the size of the previous one.

"Joseph, come on, buddy," Tommy said. "We don't care what couch you sleep on." A few more giggles, but they were murmurs, and soon enough they all went to bed. Marty took the other couch.

Early the next morning, the sound of a bus rumbling past the house. Light streaming in. Everyone slept as Joseph walked out of a house he'd considered magical for almost a year, and he'd spent a good part of another trying to re-create that magic. The porch became sand as he stepped down its wooden steps. He walked to the bus; he could no longer drive. The story, he told the few who cared, was a bad transmission. But the car still ran. The real problem is that Joseph had become deathly afraid. He thought about buying a new car, but working so he could buy another car that would take him to work so he could afford to buy another car later seemed too pointless. Joseph walked past the familiar bushes and flowers and shrubs and gardens that once seemed unique. To the U-District to catch a more direct bus, back to his place in Beacon Hill, where he lived on his own. From there, he could walk to work. On the horizon were the white-capped Cascade Mountains. The place even had a hot tub.

As it would turn out, the walking was just as bad as the driving, as Joseph had begun to worry about killing people by the way he walked, and the white-capped mountains could not be seen from the house, and the hot tub's availability was reneged by the landlord, who lived upstairs and played World of Warcraft, seemingly as a job. Walking to the bus, Joseph thought about The One. He searched for her still. Maybe the one with dreads, or the one he met up with at Red Robin in the Northgate Mall and after went to her car, or the one from Michigan who said she once kissed Jack White after a show early in his career, or the one who lived in Ravenna and tasted like ash, or the red-haired one from Utah, or the blond one with curls. Joseph got on the bus. He closed his eyes.

When he got to his rented basement floor, Joseph fell on his bed and thought about the last one. Nora Ayers ran in the same overlapping crowd of friends as Laurel and Bob and Tina and Boris and Headley. Micah first made an attempt at Nora, years before at Headley's birthday, when he said, "Joseph, I love mousy girls like Nora, you know what I mean, man?"

Joseph flipped over in bed, dreading the call he'd have to make that Saturday afternoon. Dad would ask about "the big news," but there was nothing to tell. There were only so many times he could talk about the weather. Joseph could not explain everything. He barely knew where to start.

Time still passes, and the dent keeps Joseph from sleeping. What stalls him when awake are the walks to work. He is sure he has killed someone or changed their life in some irrevocably terrible way. Every day preparing himself for work, he is crushed with the weight of knowing he has two miles with so many opportunities for tragedy. It could happen in the blink of an eye. Often he wants to think about Bethany, but mostly he is unable. Instead he thinks about the cars at the intersections, hurtling at each other. The only relief is starting work. Once in his office chair he cannot be tempted to run back out and check the places he might have hurt someone by accidentally kicking a rock or not looking enough times before he crossed a street.

The name of his boss has changed. Though none have been as bad as Mike—someone who thinks of choking small animals when he masturbates—there is still the problem of all the accrued hours put in with the old regime, going up in a cloud of smoke when another new manager comes in and Joseph has to show the new man or new woman that he is capable of handling a full-time job. Sometimes Joseph will think about moving back to South Dakota—maybe save up to buy a house in Sioux Falls—but he knows he would first have to resolve the dent, and that is something he cannot do. He also thinks of maybe going to Chicago, where William became a doctor. There would be a new set of faces there, different from the ones in Seattle.

Everyone moved on. Darrin and Crystal married and moved to the suburbs, and so did Tina and Bob. Bethany and Jeff are still together, but they stayed in the city. Headley moved to New York City, drinking unique craft beers every night. Boris moved to Washington, DC, and lives with a friend from his Air Force days. Laurel moved to Madison to build a house with her dad, while Jennifer ended up in the Twin Cities before either Joseph or she said anything about love. Micah is in Amsterdam.

Joseph knows what he will think about on his deathbed. He still has the piece of orange construction paper with the man's phone number, and some days he will get it out and touch it, but it seems to vibrate, as if toxic. The man lives closer now. That was the biggest reason Joseph moved to a basement room with the landlord who plays MMORPGs and bait-and-switched on the unusable hot tub. Joseph likes to think one day he will go to that nearby street and find the pickup and write that check. Sometimes, he even writes it down on his lists of things, along with getting milk, dropping off a check for the dentist, buying a specific brand of shampoo to help stem the final stages of balding. And Joseph will be very serious about it too, the pen digging into the paper, making the words "CALL THE MAN." But, before he does, thoughts spin.

"That guy is going to be pissed. He may not even live there anymore, you idiot. Are you ready to start knocking on people's doors to find who took the note?"

So Joseph lets himself off the hook, and tries to think of less consuming matters. Every so often Mary comes to mind, even Suzanne, though when Joseph is honest with himself, he knows neither remembers him as fondly as he does them. More recently, Joseph got another boss. Finally, this could be the one who grants that full-time job and allows Joseph Bethel to become the confident man his parents once dreamed he would be, back when he was a baby with his fly unzipped in the front yard. This boss will see something in Joseph and provide the salary that will resolve the old problems, and Joseph will get married and be happy and never have thoughts of everything crashing all around him because of past mistakes.

But if someone could have held Joseph's soul at birth, they'd know none of that will ever happen. So Joseph Bethel steps out his basement door. Once again, it is time for work.

www.ingramcontent.com/pod-product-compliance
Lightning Source LLC
Chambersburg PA
CBHW021152130626
46554CB00005B/1771